"How long are yo[...]

She sighed and glance[...]
were on her, and his affection was plain.

"I don't know," she murmured.

"It's been years now." He tilted his head, regarding her. "Mary…he's not coming back."

His words pierced her anew. Did he think she was daft? Did he think she hadn't thought that very thing over a thousand times?

"You don't know that…" she started.

He reached out and touched her shoulder, leaving his hand for only a moment. When he removed it, she still felt its warmth. Almost like a touch of comfort.

"Won't you come riding with me tonight?"

He'd been asking her repeatedly for months. Mark Schrock was a kind and good man. In truth, he could have any girl in the district.

But he wanted her.

She swallowed. Even though she liked Mark, she'd turned him down. Again and again and again. She and Isaac had *promised* each other. They'd pledged their love and their fidelity. How could she go back on that?

Brenda Maxfield's passion is writing. She is blessed to live part-time in Indiana, a state she shares with many Amish communities. She finds the best spices, hot cereal and cooking advice at an Amish store not too far away. She spends the rest of her time living in Costa Rica, on the central Pacific coast.

Brenda has also lived in Honduras and Grand Cayman. With her husband Paul, she has two grown children and five precious grandchildren. One of her favorite activities is exploring other cultures, and she can often be found walking the beaches of the world.

She loves getting to know her readers, so feel free to write her at contact@brendamaxfield.com.

BROKEN PROMISES
Brenda Maxfield

HARLEQUIN

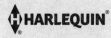

ISBN-13: 978-1-335-60512-2

Recycling programs
for this product may
not exist in your area.

Broken Promises

First published in 2017
by Tica House Publishing LLC. This edition published in 2021.

This edition published by arrangement with Harlequin Books S.A.

For questions and comments about the quality of this book,
please contact us at CustomerService@Harlequin.com.

Harlequin Enterprises ULC
22 Adelaide St. West, 40th Floor
Toronto, Ontario M5H 4E3, Canada
www.Harlequin.com

Printed in U.S.A.

BROKEN PROMISES

Chapter One

And now abideth faith, hope, and charity, these three; but the greatest of these is charity.

1 Corinthians 13:13 KJV

Mary nudged her best friend. "Well?" she whispered, keeping her eyes carefully averted.

"*Jah*, he's looking at you, just like you hoped." Deborah let out a light sigh. "You're right, Mary. He *is* handsome. I wish I had someone… *Ach*, no. He's seen me gawking at him. He's *grinning*."

Mary bit her lip to keep from laughing. Deborah shifted on the bench, her face wearing a horrified expression. "Next time, do your own snooping," she hissed in a low voice. "This is *so embarrassing*. I'm never spying for you again."

Mary dared a glimpse in Isaac's direction. Sure enough, his hazel eyes twinkled with mirth as he gave her a wink. *A wink?* Mary's breath caught, and she quickly glanced around. Had anyone seen him? But the rest of her Amish friends seemed focused on the song leader who had just started a new hymn, one of the slower more somber ones. Inwardly, Mary groaned. She preferred the faster songs—much more cheerful and definitely more fun to sing.

Isaac wasn't singing at all. He continued gazing at her, as if daring her to wink back—something she would *never* do. Imagine winking right there for everyone to see; it wasn't to be considered. But she couldn't help smiling at him. He was better than handsome. His hazel eyes, his sandy blond hair, his broad shoulders, his charming grin. She could hardly look away.

He made a motion with his head, as if inviting her outside to meet up with him. Her eyes widened, and he stifled a laugh. The boy next to him elbowed him in the ribs, and Isaac made a show of focusing on the song leader. Mary knew it was all pretense. She could see that he was still looking at her out of the corner of his eye.

She grinned. In truth, she wouldn't mind slipping outside to meet him. Of course, she wouldn't do it… And neither would he—not right in the middle of the youth singing. Tongues would wag, and the two of them would never live it down. She straightened her shoulders and sang a bit louder. The voices around her swelled, increasing in volume and fullness without the help of any instruments. A few of the people gathered in the barn were over twenty-years-old. They joined the teens every other Sunday evening…as long as they stayed single, they were welcome, so the ages of the group were mixed.

Mary liked attending. The singing and the refreshments were nice, but she didn't delude herself. Most of the attendees were mainly there to check each other out. It wasn't uncommon for couples to sneak off afterwards for a ride together in a courting buggy.

Mary's heart fluttered. Maybe Isaac would ask her to

ride with him that night. She sucked in her breath at the
possibility. Oh, how she liked him. She was tempted to
close her eyes and send up a prayer for just such an invitation, but she refrained. How could she assume that
the Lord God would be involving himself in that?

She gazed around at the group, noting that almost
all of her friends were there. When she looked over toward the empty stalls at the far corner of the barn, she
observed Mark Schrock off by himself, studying her.
She gave a slight start at the look of intensity in his
eyes. When he saw her looking back at him, he quickly
glanced away.

How odd. She wondered what he was thinking.

But she didn't have time to ponder it for long because
the singing was winding down. One more hymn, and it
would be time to drink lemonade and eat from the as-
sortment of sweets. The final song was fast and cheery,
and Mary sang with gusto. She noted that Isaac had
joined in, too, his chest expanding with fervor.

When the song was over, she and Deborah moved to
the table for refreshments. Deborah grabbed her arm.
"He's coming over," she whispered into Mary's ear.

Mary drew in a long breath and tried to calm her
racing heart, but to no avail. "You're sure?" she murmured back.

"Hi, Mary," Isaac interrupted, approaching them.
He gave her a wide smile and reached around her for a
cookie. "How are you?"

"F-fine," Mary answered, looking into his eyes. She
saw the invitation there, completely readable. She took a
cookie for herself and gave Deborah a meaningful look.
Then she hesitated. *Had* she read his unspoken offer cor-
rectly? And if so, what was she supposed to do about it?

Shaking slightly at her own nerve, she slowly moved away, heading toward the double-wide barn doors, which had been left open. She hoped with every breath inside her that she was doing the right thing. She slipped outside and paused near the row of buggies and pony carts.

Within minutes, Isaac joined her. With a laugh, he tossed his cookie aside and grabbed her hand. She tossed her cookie to the ground, too. He began running, pulling her to a thick stand of trees to the west of the barn. She stopped beside him in the shadows.

"Mary Hochstetler," he said, facing her. He continued to hold her hand. The air was still, and the shadows of light played across his face.

"Isaac Studer," she said back.

"I don't suppose you'd want a ride home tonight?"

She saw the slight quiver of his lip, betraying his nervousness. But his eyes didn't waver on hers. She swallowed past the excitement working its way up her throat.

"*Jah*, I would," she said, wanting to throw her arms up with joy. He'd *asked her*.

"Would you like to be going now, or do you want to join the group for a while longer?" He gave her a slow grin, and his grip on her hand tightened.

"Give me one minute, all right?" She pulled her hand free and ran back to the barn. Rushing up to Deborah, she yanked her away from the crowd.

"Did he ask you to ride with him?" Deborah asked breathlessly, her dark eyes gleaming.

"*Jah*," Mary answered, her own eyes wide. "We're leaving now. Go on home without me."

"You're so lucky."

Mary's heart swelled. "I know. *I know!*" And with that, she dashed back out of the barn, skirting around the clumps of youth standing about visiting. She wondered which other couples would be riding together that night. *Couples...*

Were she and Isaac a *couple?*

The evening air bit at her as she looked about for Isaac, but she hardly felt the cold. She was flushed with warmth, and all she could think of was the fine-looking boy waiting for her.

"Over here," he called out softly.

She looked to her side and saw one of the buggies ready to go. The door was open. She ran over and climbed inside, settling herself on his left.

"Ready?" he asked.

She nodded, and off they went.

"I've been meaning to ask you to ride with me for a long time," he confessed. "I'm glad you said you'd come."

The buggy tilted slightly as it left the drive onto the road. She felt a sudden shyness. She'd never been riding with a boy, and she'd never dreamed that her first time would be with someone as popular and well-liked as Isaac. As they started down the road, she glanced out the window. To her left, she thought she saw something move. She leaned to the side and pressed her face to the window. What was it? An animal? A person? Was someone *watching* them? A strange feeling snaked its way up her spine, but she dismissed it.

She turned back to Isaac and smiled.

"How about Edmund's Pond?" he suggested.

She nodded. She'd been to Edmund's Pond hundreds of times, but never with a boy.

"It might be cold."

"I don't care," she said quickly.

He chuckled and snapped the reins. The buggy moved faster. He put both reins in one hand and put his other hand on her shoulder. "I can keep you warm," he said, his voice deep.

She gulped. "O...kay," she said.

He laughed. "*Ach*, Mary, you are priceless."

"What do you mean?"

"Just what I said." He slung his arm around her and squeezed her against his side.

Priceless? He thought she was priceless? She smiled into the dark and relaxed. He was pretty priceless himself.

They talked and laughed all the way to the pond, about anything and everything. By the time Isaac looped the reins and they got out, Mary felt like she'd known him well for years.

"Can I call you Ike?" she asked on a whim.

"Nobody else does."

"*Gut.* I'll be the only one then." She grinned up at him, and he stopped to consider her. She felt strange as he studied her, his eyes resting on every feature of her face.

He touched her lower lip gently with his fingers. "And I shall call you Maria."

"Maria?"

"*Jah.* That's Mary in Spanish."

"Spanish?"

"It's all right, isn't it?" His eyes were dark and luminous in the moonlight.

"Of course," she whispered.

He took her hand. "*Gut.* Shall we walk around the pond?"

"*Jah.*"

And they did, talking the entire way. When they returned to the buggy, Mary had no idea how much time had passed. But she knew that her folks wouldn't question her—they would assume she'd been out with a boy. Nor would they ask her who it was. Such things were kept private.

Mary pressed her hands to her chest all the way home. Her heart was beating out of control. She glanced at Isaac and saw him looking at her. He was *the one*. She knew it to the soles of her feet.

He was the one. *Isaac Studer*.

Chapter Two

Isaac waited nearly every day for Mary at the end of her drive. He'd stand behind the thick maple tree just off the road. When she'd appear, he'd grab her hand, and they'd run to the thick stand of trees in front of her father's fields. No one could see them there. Isaac fashioned a bench of sorts, out of a fallen log. They sat for hours, talking and laughing, always careful to keep quiet if someone passed by.

Mary lived for those clandestine meetings. She loved everything about Isaac and could never seem to get enough of him.

"Maria, I have something to tell you," he told her one late afternoon.

At first, she smiled. But then she saw something in his eyes that sent shivers up her spine. "What is it?"

He took her hands in his, but he kept his eyes down. She waited, and her breath went shallow.

"What is it?" she asked again. "You're scaring me…"

She watched him swallow and saw his jaw tighten.

"I'm leaving."

"What?"

"*Nee*, not for *gut*," he said quickly, now looking at her again. "Just for a while."

"What do you mean?" She'd gone stiff, her eyes glued to his.

"You know I never went on my *rumspringa*."

She gaped at him. "You've never said a thing about going on one. You never—"

He let go of her hands. "I've been thinking about it for a long time."

"But you never said—"

"I know. I know." He rubbed his thighs as if trying to wipe something off his hands. "But I have the chance to go visit my cousin."

"Your cousin? Well, that wouldn't be much of a *rumspringa*, would it? Where does he live? Ohio?"

"*Jah*." He swallowed again. "But the thing is, he went fancy."

Her heart froze. She licked her lips. "What?"

"He went fancy, and he wants me to stay with him for a while."

"He's *Englisch*?"

Isaac nodded. He grabbed her hands again. "Haven't you ever wondered, Maria? Haven't you ever wondered what we're missing? What's out there? What it's like?"

She was so stunned, she couldn't speak.

"Say something," he said. "Surely, you've wondered. Surely, you have."

She pulled her hands from his. "A bit. Now and then. But not really. Not seriously."

"Well, I have." He blinked. "And now I have the chance. You know, to really see for myself. Before I'm baptized into the church."

Her heart lurched. "But I thought you were going to be baptized in November."

He chewed the edge of his lip. "*Nee*. I never said that."

"But we've talked about it!"

"*You* talked about it. I never said I would."

Mary's mind spun. Was that true? Had he never said he was going to be baptized? Had she just assumed? She desperately tried to remember.

"It'll be all right," he whispered. "I just need to go for a while. I'll come back. Of course, I'll come back. For you."

Her eyes misted over. She felt like she was going to vomit. The earth was spinning out of control.

"I'll come back, and we'll be together forever," he assured her, his voice thick with emotion. "As soon as I come back, we'll be married. Maybe in a year. We're still young."

"I'm almost eighteen," she said, surprised her voice even worked.

"I know."

"Have you told your parents? Are you really going?"

He nodded. "A van is picking me up tomorrow."

"Tomorrow?" She nearly choked.

"I didn't want to tell you sooner. I thought it'd be easier this way."

"Ike…" she whispered.

He grabbed her up into his arms, pressing her head on his shoulder. She felt his heart beating rapidly beneath her cheek.

"I'll come back," he promised. "You'll wait for me, won't you?"

She began to cry then, muffled sobs against his coat.

"*Ach*, Maria, don't cry."

She buried her face into him.

"*Ach*, Maria. Please stop."

He drew back and put his finger under her chin, lifting her face to his. He leaned forward and kissed her gently on the mouth. His lips were soft and cool and light.

She blinked rapidly, trying to stop her tears. But it was no use.

They continued to fall.

Mary could barely function the next day. Her mind played the night before over and over and over. She kept looking at the clock. Was he gone now? Had the van already come for him? Or was he waiting on his porch? Maybe the van was coming in the afternoon.

By supper time, she knew he was surely gone. He'd told her he would write. But, would he? She blew her nose for the hundredth time. *Of course*, he would. He always kept his promises, didn't he? Which also meant he would come back for her.

"You getting sick?" her mother asked her. "You been sniffling around all day."

Mary stuffed her handkerchief beneath the waistband of her apron. "*Nee*. I'm fine."

"You don't sound fine."

Her brother John came into the kitchen. "Ain't supper ready, yet?"

Sandra Hochstetler gave him a mock grimace. "Out with you, son. We'll be serving when we're serving."

John laughed and left the room.

"Mary, fetch the bowl of potatoes. I think everything's ready but the beans. I'll be bringing them in."

Mary picked up the heavy glass bowl and took it out

to the table. Her four brothers were already sitting there, waiting. Her father came in from the front room.

"Smells *gut*," he said.

Her mother brought in the beans. When everyone was settled, her father bowed his head. "Shall we pray?"

There was silence around the table. Mary prayed for Isaac, for his safety, for his speedy return. The year before, Frances Yordy had left on her *rumspringa* and never returned. Her mother wouldn't discuss it, but Mary had overheard the women talking. Frances had gotten involved in some music group. She had learned to play the drums and the last thing anyone knew, she was traveling the country, frequenting bars and other shady venues. The women had talked about her with a heaviness that had made Mary want to cry.

Would the same thing happen to Isaac? Would he find some other interest that would pull him away from Hollybrook permanently? She shuddered with dread.

Her father cleared his throat, indicating that the silent blessing was over. Everyone looked up, and the bowls of food began making their way around the table. Mary could feel her mother's sharp eyes on her, so she intentionally kept her own gaze focused on her plate. But she could barely get down more than a bite or two.

"After supper, you go on up to your room and lie down," her mother said.

Mary looked at her. "*Nee, Mamm*. I'm fine."

"If she goes up, she'll miss our nightly Bible reading," her father countered.

"She's coming down with something," Sandra said, pursing her lips. "I'll *red* up the kitchen by myself." She glanced at her sons. "Or get one of you to help me."

There was a general cry of protest, and then her brothers started teasing each other.

Mary sighed. This meal couldn't get over fast enough.

Chapter Three

Three Years Later...

Mark Schrock stood outside the Feed & Supply, leaning his tall frame against the side of the building. Mary saw him and cringed, but it was too late to turn back... Besides, how ridiculous would that look? Climbing back into her pony cart and leaving when she'd just arrived? Resolutely, she squared her shoulders and attempted to pass him without speaking.

"How long are you going to wait?" he asked as she drew even with him.

She paused, not looking at him.

"Mary?" He spoke her name softly.

She sighed and glanced up. His clear blue eyes were on her, and his affection was plain.

"I don't know," she murmured.

"It's been years now." He tilted his head, regarding her. "Mary...he's not coming back."

His words pierced her anew. Did he think she was daft? Did he think she hadn't thought that very thing over a thousand times? But Isaac had promised her.

He had *promised* to come back for her. Promised to marry her.

"You don't know that…" she started.

He reached out and touched her shoulder, leaving his hand for only a moment. When he removed it, she still felt its warmth. Almost like a touch of comfort. Tears filled her eyes.

"Won't you come riding with me tonight?"

He'd been asking her repeatedly for months. She knew he was smitten with her. She knew he was waiting for her to get over Isaac. For the past three years, he'd been biding his time, and she had to admire his dogged persistence. Mark Schrock was a kind and good man. In truth, he could have any girl in the district.

But he wanted her.

She swallowed. Even though she liked Mark, she'd turned him down. Again and again and again. She and Isaac had *promised* each other. They'd pledged their love and their fidelity. How could she go back on that?

She looked down at her hands and absently picked at a hangnail on her thumb.

"Mary?"

She licked her lips and looked up at him. His expression was so sincere, so full of sympathy and eagerness, that her breath caught. He was a good-looking man. Tall and slender, with strong arms and a certain smile that despite everything, appealed to her. Was he telling the truth? Was it time for her to let go? To get on with her life?

Her best friend Deborah had been married for a year and a half. She already had one child and was probably expecting her second by now. Many of her other friends had been courting for months—or at least, everything indicated as much.

Mark cleared his throat. He hadn't moved. He was waiting…

Perhaps if she went riding with him once, he'd quit pressuring her. Perhaps, it would get her out of his system.

She nodded.

He straightened his shoulders and stared. "Did you just nod?"

"Maybe…" she said almost playfully, and then felt her face go hot. What was she *doing*? Flirting with him now? Just like that?

"I'll be at the end of your drive at seven tonight," he said quickly. And then, probably thinking she might change her mind, he left immediately, giving her no chance to do so.

Mary watched him leave. He nearly leapt into his wagon, and without a backward glance, he was out of the expansive parking area and on his way down the road.

Mary did her shopping quickly and set out for home. These days, she kept to herself as much as possible, which granted, usually only meant she had a few moments to herself during the afternoon. But today, she sneaked away to her room upstairs and closed her door. If her mother came up, she'd wonder at that, but Mary closed it anyway. Then she went to her bed and sat down. She leaned over and opened the drawer of her bedside table. She pulled out a small handful of letters.

Isaac's letters. They were tattered and the addresses on the fronts of the envelopes were faded from handling.

He'd written her during those first few weeks he was gone. She'd received seven letters in total.

Seven letters in three years.

She'd read each letter so many times that she knew each word by heart. Pressing them to her chest, she swallowed back her tears. She was pathetic. There was no other term for it. What girl in her right mind waited three years for a boy who had stopped writing after a few weeks?

A pathetic, sad, delusional girl. That was who. She tossed the letters on her quilt and jumped up from the bed, stalking across the room to her window. She rested her head against the window frame and let out a long shaky breath.

What was Isaac doing right then? In his *Englisch* world? And who was he courting? A jagged pain sliced through her heart. A man as handsome and charming as Isaac Studer would be courting someone. That she knew.

Only that someone wasn't her. Not anymore. She closed her eyes and felt the prickle of tears against her lashes. Mark was right. It was time to let go. Once and for all, let go. She opened her eyes and brushed her tears away with the back of her hand. She turned from the window and looked at her four dresses hanging on pegs near the door.

Her dark blue dress would suit for a buggy ride. She'd wear it that evening. With her new cape. She walked to her dresser and picked up her hand mirror, staring at her reflection. Her large brown eyes were still moist and luminous. Her cheeks were a bit flushed, which gave her a fresh, clean look, as if she'd just come in from the cold. But her mouth…

Her mouth was sad. She tried on a smile and then felt foolish. She set the mirror back on the dresser.

She would re-brush her hair and put on a clean *kapp* for her outing. Her outing? It was a *date*, and she'd better just get used to the idea.

"*Mamm*, I'll be stepping out this evening for a bit," Mary said as she helped with the dishes after supper.

Her mother's eyebrows rose, and she gave Mary a curious look, but she didn't question her. It wasn't their way. She only nodded and went back to scrubbing the cast iron skillet.

"I won't be long." Why Mary had felt compelled to say that, she couldn't begin to guess. It wasn't necessary. Was she informing her mother or herself? With a disgusted sigh, she rubbed the dishtowel harder over the already dry plate.

Her mother stopped scrubbing and looked at her again. "It's all right, Mary," she said in a low quiet tone. "It's all right."

Instant tears sprang to Mary's eyes. She nodded blindly and blinked hard, putting the plate into the cupboard.

Chapter Four

Mary needlessly smoothed her hair behind her ears. Her bun was completely tidy, every hair already tucked beneath her *kapp*. She glanced down at her dress and saw that it hung a bit loosely around the waist. Was she losing weight? She could hardly afford to, considering how thin she already was. Supper that evening hadn't helped as she'd hardly been able to swallow a bite of food. Well, too late to do anything about that now.

She glanced at the wind-up clock on her bedside table. Mark would be waiting for her any minute. She inhaled sharply and left her room. She hurried down the stairs and into the wash room where her new black cape hung on a peg next to the door. She put it on and debated whether to take a scarf. The evenings hadn't been too cold yet, so she opted to skip that.

Without a word to anyone in her family, she slipped out the door and walked quickly across the yard. It was dark with only the faint shine of the stars to light her way. But she'd crossed their large yard many times in total darkness, so it wasn't a problem. When she got to the road, she saw the black hulking shadow of a horse and buggy, waiting. The large orange triangle on the back was clearly visible in the dim light. Mark had also fashioned two battery-run lights on each side of the wagon, shining forward.

The door opened.

"Evening, Mary," Mark said, his voice low and melodic.

"*Gut* evening, Mark," she responded, climbing in beside him. She shut the door and without another word, they were off.

Mary let the rhythmic jostling of the buggy calm her. She was nervous, but she certainly didn't want to show it. She swallowed past her dry throat and tried to think of something to say. Her mind automatically flew backward to when she and Isaac used to ride together.

They had chatted non-stop, hardly taking a breath.

She bit her lower lip. She was not going to compare Mark to Isaac. She was *not*.

"How was your afternoon?" Mark asked, breaking the silence.

"Right fine," she answered. Her mind whirled for some topic to discuss. "Not too cold yet, is it?" she uttered and then felt ridiculous.

He chuckled softly. "I'm nervous, too," he said gently, looking over at her.

She smiled back and suddenly felt better. "Sorry."

He shook his head. "Don't be. We just need to get to know each other. That's all."

"*Jah.* That's all." And just like that, Mary relaxed and began to enjoy herself. They spoke of the stars, the crops, the busy-ness of harvesting. They spoke of the new family who'd just moved to Hollybrook from Illinois.

"Have you been?" he asked her.

"Where? Illinois?"

"*Jah.*"

"*Nee.* But I've been to Ohio a few times. How about you?"

"In truth, I've not been out of Indiana. Never had any reason to leave."

"We have family in Ohio. That's why I've been there." She twisted to face him more directly. "Have you ever wanted to travel?"

And with those words, came the image of Isaac. She remembered the gleam in his eye when he talked about exploring new places. A heaviness descended on her. Her stomach felt leaden, as if someone had drained all her energy, and she leaned against the side of the buggy.

Mark turned the buggy off the road. He pulled up on the reins and faced her. "What just happened?"

She blew out her breath. "Nothing. Nothing happened." She squirmed. Could he read her mind?

"Mary, I've been pursuing you for a while now. You know that, and I know that. I also know that you were sweet on Isaac Studer..." His voice faded, but then he spoke again, with more resonance. "If you don't want to be here with me, you don't have to be."

Her lips parted, and her chest constricted. She was sick and tired of Isaac ruining everything. It was almost as if he lived with her, always there, always hovering over her, watching everything she did, listening to everything she said. Her shoulders tensed. Had she done this? Had she created a monster out of Isaac's memory? Had she thought about him so continuously that now her very thoughts of him had trapped her?

"Mary?" Mark reached out and touched her sleeve. "Are you all right?"

The buggy was closing in on her. It was too small. There wasn't any air. She yanked on the door handle and tumbled outside. She leaned back against the buggy and took huge gulping breaths. She heard Mark's door open, and then he was beside her.

"What is it? Are you sick?" he asked, his voice thick with worry.

She nodded. "*Jah*." She nearly gagged. "I'm sick. I'm sick."

"Do you need to vomit? Should I take you home?"

She held up her hand. "*Nee*. Give me a minute…" She rested her head back against the cool surface of the buggy. She closed her eyes and took deliberate, even breaths. Her hammering heart slowed. She didn't move. The wave of nausea passed, leaving a dull throbbing throughout her body.

"I'm sorry," she whispered.

"No need to be," Isaac answered, his voice gentle. "What can I do for you?"

She wanted to ask him to hold her, to rub her back, to let her lean on his shoulder. But she could hardly do that. She only looked at him, knowing her eyes were wide and filled with tears.

Why had she never seen it before? Why had she gone three *years* without understanding what she was doing to herself? She had thought she was being faithful to Isaac. Loyal. Patient.

And maybe, in the beginning, that *was* what she had been doing. But as the months went by, as day after day after day went by with no more news, no more letters, it had morphed into something entirely different. Her faithfulness had become a trap. A sort of jail.

"Mark?"

"*Jah*?" He stepped closer.

"Can we walk a bit?"

"*Jah*, of course. Let me secure the reins."

She loved that he didn't question her. That he didn't wonder why she suddenly wanted to walk along the side of the road. Within seconds, he was back at her side, and they began to walk. There was a smattering of street lights, but even so, the area was mostly shrouded in shadows. Mark held her elbow as they moved down the road.

"I'm sorry about that."

"Sorry about what?" he asked.

"About being nauseous. Feeling sick."

He stopped her. His dark figure loomed tall. She could see a shimmer of light in his eyes as he looked at her. "Mary, you never have to apologize for something like that. I only hope you're feeling better."

He was so close to her. So near. She could almost feel his breath. The world around them went silent. She could hear nothing but her own heartbeat pounding in her ears. She stood as if transfixed, gazing up into his shadowed face.

And then he leaned down and touched his lips gently to her cheek. He lingered for a moment, and she felt his warmth on her. A trembling filled her. A yearning to be cradled. To be cherished. To be loved.

"Mary," he whispered, his mouth close to her ear.

She didn't breathe. Didn't move.

And then she was in his arms. He held her close, resting his chin on her head. Though he was thin, she felt his strength, his vigor, and his goodness. She bit her lip to stifle an involuntary cry.

"It's all right," he murmured. "Everything is all right."

She squeezed her eyes shut and leaned into him,

clinging to his words. Choosing to believe him. They stood like that, pressed together, for a long while. Finally, he gently pulled free and gazed down at her.

"Are you okay?"

She nodded, realizing with stunned clarity that she was. For the first time in three years, she felt freedom edging its way into her heart.

"We haven't really courted," he said.

She blinked. "What?"

"I want to be married."

Her lips parted, and she felt as if her breath had been cut off. "What?" she repeated.

"We're not teens anymore. I'm twenty-three. I've loved you for years, Mary." He gazed at her in the darkness. "Mary, I love you. I've always loved you."

He hesitated, and she felt his sudden nervousness. She'd always known he was interested in her. But *loved* her? That, she hadn't known.

"I know that you don't love me. Not yet. But I want to be married. You're a beautiful girl, Mary. A fine person. I will do everything I can to make you happy." He grasped both her hands. "Please say you will."

She couldn't move. Couldn't take her eyes from his face. She wished for more light so she could see him better. So she could see every feature of his face, so she could look deeply into his eyes. Strangely, she felt calm. Even peaceful. She wondered at that. Wondered how she could be so serene considering what he'd just asked.

And then it became clear to her, and she knew what she was going to do. What she was going to answer.

"*Jah*," she murmured, stepping closer to him again. Here was a man she could trust. Here was a man who loved her. "*Jah*. I will marry you."

As soon as the words were out, she felt right. She would marry this wonderful man who stood before her. She would be his wife. And she would work to be the best wife she could possibly be. She smiled at the wonder of it all. She didn't stop to analyze it. She didn't stop to weigh all the possibilities. She didn't stop to question the suddenness of her acceptance.

She only let herself feel the joy of it wash over her.

"*Ach*, Mary!" Mark grabbed her to him once again, pressing her against his chest with joyous exuberance.

She laughed into his coat.

"You'll grow to love me," he said. "You'll see. We'll be so happy."

She tightened her arms around him. "I know," she murmured. "I know."

Chapter Five

But Mark had been wrong.

Mary hadn't grown to love him. At least, not in the way that he had meant. She tried. Oh, *how* she tried.

Months after they were married, she continued to wait for it—that tingle of excitement, that exuberance and joy she wanted to feel in her husband's presence. But it didn't come.

Mark was a good man, just as good and upright and steady as she had predicted. He was loving and kind and thoughtful. But as the days wore on and Mary failed to respond to him in the way he'd hoped, his demeanor changed.

A sadness came to his step. A heaviness filled his voice and his mood. Mark had always been quick to help someone in the community. Now, he seemed desperate to be the very first one to show up at any sign of need. He helped men work on their buggies. He rushed to the aid of anyone hurt or ill. He suggested barn raisings, even though the weather had turned cold with crunchy frost greeting them every morning.

He was driven.

Mary watched him and worried. She knew what was happening—if he couldn't get what he needed at home, he'd find it elsewhere. She worked hard to say the right things to him. She told him thank you a million times a week.

"Thank you for fixing the chicken coop. It looks fine, now."

"Thank you for fetching flour from the Feed & Supply. I certainly needed it."

"Thank you for nailing that new board onto the porch. Now, I won't have to worry about falling through." She'd added a laugh at the end of that comment, but he hadn't responded.

Now, she stood at her bedroom window in the small farmhouse they were leasing. She could see the barn from the window, and she watched for signs of Mark. He'd taken to spending more and more time in the barn, and she suspected there weren't that many chores out there.

The harvest had been taken in, and the only thing left in the garden were pumpkins and some hardy squash. They'd already dug up the potatoes. There simply wasn't that much to do outside anymore. And even if he was sharpening the plow and seasoning the leather, he would have been long finished by then.

She sighed heavily and put on her *kapp*. He was avoiding her as much as possible.

This couldn't go on. It simply couldn't.

Every day, she felt like a failure. Every day, she yearned to feel more for him.

And every day, images of Isaac filled her heart and mind. She tried to chase them away. She prayed almost continually for her thoughts and feelings to go away. But, they remained—a part of her that she simply couldn't get rid of. Couldn't cut off.

It was *miserable*.

"Mary?"

Mary gave a start and whirled around to see Mark at the bedroom door. So, he hadn't been out in the barn.

"Jah?" she asked, gasping softly.

"Did I scare you? I didn't mean to."

She looked into his familiar face, at the blue eyes that used to twinkle, at the mouth she rarely saw smile anymore. *"Nee.* It's fine. I thought you were in the barn."

He stepped into the room, and she noticed again how tall he was. He looked down at her. "I'm thinking that maybe I should head up north and go to the auction."

"You mean the horse auction? Do we need another horse?"

He shifted his weight from one foot to the other and rubbed his hand over his newly grown beard. "Wouldn't hurt to look," he said.

She regarded him. He was uncomfortable, ill at ease. With *her*—his own wife. They didn't need a new horse. She was sure of it. Nor could they really afford one.

"You hiring a van?" she asked.

"Jah. Some of the neighbor men are heading up there. I thought I'd join them."

"You staying the night?"

He shrugged. "Doubt it."

"That's a long day then."

"Jah, it is."

They gazed at each other. The tension in the room mounted until Mary thought she'd need an axe to chop through it. Tears burned the back of her eyelids.

"Well, then, I hope you have a *gut* trip."

He stared at her until she wanted to squirm. Finally, she could stand it no more. She burst into tears and sank down on the edge of the bed. In one stride, he was beside her, sitting next to her, holding her somewhat stiffly in his arms.

"*Ach*, Mary. What is it?"

She gulped her tears and drew back to look at him. "It's nothing. I'm all right."

"How can it be nothing?" he asked, inching slightly away.

"I'll just… I'll miss you is all."

The look of hope on his face nearly broke her heart. She sniffed and wiped at her eyes. Had she just lied to him? Lied right to his face? She looked down at her lap, her mind grasping for something, anything. She did like him. She *did*. But she wouldn't miss him. How could she, when his very presence kept reminding her of what they didn't have?

"I won't be long…" He brushed his knuckles over her cheek. "I don't have to go."

She swallowed hard over the lump in her throat. "*Nee*. You go on. Go ahead and go. It'll probably be right interesting."

He stiffened, and she couldn't bear it. She leaned forward and stretched herself up to kiss him. At first, he didn't respond, and then, he kissed her back with such hunger that her breath froze in her throat. He put his arms around her and crushed her to him, his mouth taking hers. She clung to him, wanting to make him feel better. Wanting to make him not regret marrying her. Wanting to fix things between them.

She squeezed her eyes shut against the vision of Isaac

and concentrated on her husband. He loved her. She could feel it in every movement he made. He loved her.

It *had* to be enough.

Mary refastened her dress and put on her apron. Mark stood by the bed, watching her. She kept her eyes averted, feeling suddenly shy and embarrassed. She scoffed inwardly. There was nothing to be embarrassed about...

So then, why was she? Why did she feel such a desperate need to leave the room, perhaps even to leave the house? A desperate need to go somewhere. *Anywhere.*

Mark cleared his throat. "You all right?"

She looked at him then, and put on a small smile. "*Jah.* Of course. I'm fine." Her words were clipped, and she hated the way they echoed through the gaping space between them.

He nodded, and pulled a suspender over his shoulder. "I'll be busy outside," he muttered. He passed her, pausing for a brief second to look into her eyes, and then with a sigh, he left the room.

Mary collapsed onto the mussed quilt. She pressed her hand to her mouth and held back her tears.

Chapter Six

After the Sunday service, Mary helped the women in the Lapps' kitchen organize the food to carry out to the barn. Her mother stepped close and looked at her.

"You all right, daughter?"

Mary frowned. "Of course. Why wouldn't I be?"

"You have a different look about you today. You feeling peaked?"

"*Nee.* I'm fine." Mary set two fresh loaves of bread on a tray. In truth, she *wasn't* feeling fine. She suspected that she had a minor case of stomach flu, but she wasn't about to tell her mother. Sandra Hochstetler tended to be a bit overdramatic when someone felt under the weather. Mary picked up the tray and hustled through the side door out to the barn. She had been careful to wash her hands and keep from breathing on the food, figuring she was probably contagious.

In any case, there was work to be done. The men were already seated at the long row of tables. When they finished their meal, the children and women would eat as there wasn't room to feed everyone at once. Mary glanced over to where her husband stood talking with some of the men. He was laughing and gesturing with his hands. She stood for a moment, transfixed. He used to be that animated with her.

But not anymore. Especially following that morning two weeks before. He'd hardly touched her since. Had their time together been that horrible for him? She winced. Was there something wrong with her?

"Mary, did you hear?" Deborah Zook walked up to her.

"Hear what?"

Deborah's expression tightened. "If you have to ask, then you haven't heard."

"What are you talking about?"

Deborah pulled her aside, then led her all the way outside the barn. She stopped amidst the buggies.

"Isaac Studer is coming home."

Mary's stomach heaved. *What?*

"Isaac Studer is coming home," she repeated.

Mary's knees buckled, and Deborah reached out and grabbed her. "Mary!"

Blackness clouded the edges of Mary's vision, and the ground shifted beneath her. She leaned heavily on her friend and fought the nausea rising in her throat, but she couldn't stop it. She lurched away from Deborah and bending double, she vomited alongside the wheel of a buggy.

"Mary!" Deborah cried again.

Mary fell back against the buggy, struggling for breath.

"*Ach*, Mary. I shouldn't have told you. I didn't think you'd… *Ach*, Mary!"

Mary shook her head and gulped in air. "It's all right. I've been sick."

Deborah slipped off her apron and used it to mop Mary's face. Then she kicked dirt over the vomit on the ground.

"No one needs to know," she whispered. She looked at Mary. "I'm so sorry. Have you really been sick?"

Mary looked down to make sure she hadn't soiled her dress. "I've been sick," she confirmed.

Deborah grabbed her arm. "We're best friends, Mary. I know we don't see each other as much now that we're both married, but still. What's going on? You've not been yourself for months."

Mary didn't answer. She only looked down.

"Is it Isaac? You still love him, don't you?"

Mary bit her lower lip. She looked at Deborah with tears in her eyes. "*Nee*. I don't. I *can't*. I have the kindest husband in the world. I can't love anyone but Mark." Her voice rose in pitch, and Deborah pulled her farther into the row of buggies.

"We can't always help how we feel." She stared at Mary. "Have you prayed about it?"

Mary gave her a helpless look. "A million times."

Deborah rubbed her hand on her forehead. "*Gott* won't desert you. He'll help you. I know he will."

Mary nodded her head. "*Jah*. He'll help me." She spoke the words, but she didn't really mean them. Lately, she felt that God wasn't helping her at all.

"Maybe you won't have to see Isaac."

Mary grimaced. "How? How can I avoid seeing him? It's not like our district has thousands and thousands of people in it. I'll see him." Another wave of weakness passed through her, and she worked to stay upright.

Deborah sighed. "But, maybe you won't—"

"When is he coming? And why? Why, now?"

"I don't know. I only heard his sister Betty talking about him at the Feed & Supply. I guess he's coming back for *gut*."

"Is he bringing…a wife?"

Deborah scowled. "Not that I know of. But Mary, you can't even wonder something like that."

"I know."

"You have to put him out of your mind. You *have* to."

"I know."

"It's been years now. *Years*. It's over with him." Deborah's voice took on a pleading quality.

"I know that." Mary squared her shoulders. "I know, Deborah. I'm not stupid. It's over. It's been over between us for years. I've moved on with my life."

Deborah squeezed her arm. "*Jah*. You have. And so has he. Remember that, Mary."

"I don't need reminding…"

Deborah loosened her grip. "Of course, you don't. I'm sorry. I'm not being helpful, am I?"

Mary shuddered. "It's fine. You're fine. I'm going to be all right. I'm glad you warned me. I don't know what I would have done if I'd…well…if I'd suddenly seen him without any warning."

"So, I was right to tell you?"

"You were right."

"I was worried about it…" Deborah tilted her head. "We should be getting back. Are you going to be okay if we go back?"

Mary swallowed with effort. "*Jah*. Let's go."

They walked back inside the barn, but the queasiness in Mary's stomach didn't let up.

Chapter Seven

During the next days, Mary attacked her house with vigor. She went at the cleaning as if it were spring, instead of coming on winter. She scrubbed until her hands were raw and her back cried out in pain. Every night, she fell into bed exhausted. She turned in before Mark and didn't even know when he came to bed.

When she awoke in the mornings, he would already be gone. She knew he'd been there because the quilts were jumbled on his side. Other than that, there was no evidence of his presence.

Things between them remained awkward. Mary tried to offer bits of conversation during the meals. He answered her, but didn't offer much else. They mostly ate quietly; the scrape of the utensils against their plates was the only sound.

On Thursday, Mary got out of bed, dressed, and went downstairs to find Mark sitting at the kitchen table. He was drinking a cup of coffee.

"*Ach*," she fussed. "I would have made that for you."

"You were asleep."

"I'm awake now. I'll get your breakfast right quick."

He watched her. She could feel his eyes follow her every move. More than once, she glanced over at him and gave him a smile. He barely nodded in return.

"I'm leaving tomorrow. Early."

"The horse auction?"

"*Jah*. The van will pick me up between six and seven."

Mary broke four eggs into a bowl and began whipping them. "You'll have a *gut* time."

"A *gut* time…" His voice faded.

She squirmed slightly and didn't look at him. She hauled the cast iron frying pan from the drawer below the oven and put it on the burner. She plopped a blob of butter into it and turned on the gas. Within seconds, the butter was sizzling and popping and sliding around the pan. She poured in the eggs, and they hissed and steamed.

"Mary?"

She grabbed the rubber spatula and looked at him. "*Jah*?"

"You been feeling well?"

She stirred the eggs. "I thought I had a touch of the flu, but I'm feeling better now."

He stood and took his mug over to place it in the sink. "You've been doin' spring cleaning around the place."

She gave a small laugh. "I was in the mood."

"Looks nice around here."

"Thank you. Your eggs are nearly ready. I can fry up some potatoes if you like." She frowned. What was she thinking? She should have cooked the potatoes first.

"*Nee*. Eggs and toast are fine." He looked at the undisturbed loaf of bread. "I'll get the baking sheet."

Honestly, she wasn't thinking straight that morning. She should have put the slices into the oven right away.

She guessed it was a good thing he'd made his own coffee.

"I'm heading over to the Yoders this morning after I finish up with the animals. It's getting harder and harder for Isaiah to take care of his equipment. I thought to help him."

She nodded. "That's right nice of you."

He grimaced and turned away. "The eggs are burning."

She jerked her head toward the smoking skillet. "*Ach*!" she cried, grabbing the handle. She slid the pan off the cook stove and onto the counter.

"Mary! You'll burn yourself!" He hurried to her and grabbed her hand.

Everything switched into slow motion. She watched him bend over her and inspect her skin carefully for burns. Then she watched him draw her hand to his mouth and gently kiss each of her fingertips. Her fingers smarted, but his cool lips soothed them, slowly, one by one. He paused, her hand still at his mouth. He looked at her and something dark burned in his eyes. Neither of them moved. Neither of them spoke. Her throat went dry.

And then he coughed, and it was over. He awkwardly let go of her, and her hand dropped to her side. He stepped back, and she saw him swallow.

"I'm not hungry," he muttered and left the room.

She stood still, watching him retreat. The smell of burnt eggs soured the air. She breathed in and out, staring through the empty door frame. What had just happened?

A wave of nausea surged up her throat, and she leaned over the sink and vomited.

* * *

The next morning, Mary fastened her cape beneath her chin. Mark was long gone; the van having picked him up at six-thirty-five. He'd given her a peck on the cheek and walked out the door. She'd immediately busied herself in the kitchen until the walls started to close in on her. She was lonely. Strangely, she missed the noise of her childhood household. And she missed her best friend.

She knew Deborah would be busy that morning, but she didn't care. She would stop over and help in any way she could. When she stepped outside, the cold air grabbed her and she let out a gasp. She saw the frost glistening on the grass and wondered just how cold it had gotten the night before.

No matter. She could hunker down inside her heavy cape, and she'd be fine. On second thought, she dashed back into the wash room and grabbed a scarf and some mittens. She didn't put the mittens on yet as hitching up a pony with them on, was nigh to impossible. She scurried across the yard to the barn and went inside, taking Flame from his stall. Her fingers went slowly numb as she set about hitching him up. By the time she climbed up onto the bench, she thought they'd crack with the cold. She put on her mittens and then slapped the reins gently on Flame's backside.

"Let's go, boy."

Flame got right into motion. The horse seemed to enjoy the cold, and his breath heaved, forming white clouds puffing up from his nostrils as he trotted along. Mary relaxed. If she kept her mouth closed and her head slightly down, the cold didn't bite so badly.

It didn't take long to arrive at Deborah's. She drove

right up to the expansive front porch and climbed down. She secured the reins and went to the front door. She knocked, even though she knew knocking wasn't common. For some reason that day, she felt hesitant to barge right in.

The door swung open, and there stood Deborah, balancing little Ross on her hip. "Mary!" she cried, obviously delighted. "Come right on in."

"Thanks," Mary said, reaching out to tousle Ross's hair.

"What brings you so early?"

"Mark went to auction, and... I don't know, I felt a bit alone."

"*Jah*. I heard some of the men were taking a van up north. I didn't know you and Mark were in need of another horse."

"We aren't," Mary said.

Deborah's eyebrow cocked. "Oh?"

Mary looked around, ensuring no one else was about. "In truth, I think he wanted a break from me."

Deborah set Ross down on the braided rug. "*Ach, nee.* Is this still about Isaac?"

Mary shook her head. "It's about me."

"You?"

"Can we talk of something else? My brain seems to be stuck in a rut deeper than Edmund's Pond."

Deborah laughed. "We can. Want to help me with the ironing?" At Mary's questioning look, she raised her hand. "Please. I don't want to hear about it. I know it should have been done on Tuesday, but here we are."

She had the ironing board set up in the kitchen, close to the warming stove. There was a large basket full of rumpled clothes beside it.

"I have a better idea," Mary said. "You sit in the rocker, and I'll do the ironing."

"*Nee*, that's not what I meant."

"I know it isn't. But you can use the break. Admit it."

Deborah chuckled. "Oh, I have no problem admitting it." She sank down into the rocker and let out her breath in a loud sigh. "I'm happy to rest these weary, over-worked bones."

"You're expecting again, Deborah. I imagine your bones are going to get even wearier before you're done."

Deborah laughed again. "I expect so."

Mary licked her finger and barely touched it to the iron. The iron let out a hiss. She pulled one of Deborah's husband's shirts from the pile and arranged it on the ironing board. Then she began pressing one of the sleeves. She hadn't gotten far when the iron grew too cold to be effective. She set it back on the stove and removed the handle, slipping it onto the second iron which was now heated nicely.

"I'm thinking about getting one of them irons that use gas. You just fill them up and then regulate the flames to the heat you want."

"Sounds like a lot of fuss," Mary said. "I don't mind using this type. Still works fine."

"For sure and for certain, that type works fine. But I'd still like to try one of them gas ones."

Mary smiled. "You let me know how you like it."

Deborah pressed on her belly and watched Ross crawl about on the floor. "This new *boppli* kicks up a storm," she said.

Mary paused in her work and looked at her friend.

Deborah continued. "You want to feel her?"

"Her?"

"Or him. But, it's a girl babe. I just know it. Come here. Put your hand right here." Deborah indicated the side of her stomach.

Mary put her hand where Deborah pointed and felt a quick jab. She grinned. "*Ach*, she's a strong one."

"That she is." Deborah glanced again at Ross. "She's going to give her big brother grief."

Mary concentrated again on her ironing. It was pleasant chatting again with Deborah. She'd been right to come. This was certainly better than sitting at home, letting her disturbing thoughts rule her life.

She stayed long enough to eat the noon meal with Deborah. Her husband Eli came in for the meal, and the three of them visited amicably. Ross sat in his high chair, smooshing his food around on the tray. Mary was surprised that he got any of it into his mouth.

After *redding* up the kitchen, Mary prepared to take her leave.

"Thank you for coming," Deborah said. "And thank you for ironing. It was a *gut* morning."

"*Jah*, it was." Mary fastened her cape under her chin and pulled on her mittens.

"Don't forget your scarf."

"Oh, right," Mary said, taking it from Deborah's hands. "I'll be back again soon," she promised.

"You do that."

With a smile and a nod, Mary left the house. She knew that Eli had seen to Flame, both unhitching him earlier and re-hitching him now for her. She was grateful, for after the cheery warmth of the house, it felt bleak and unfriendly outside, and she was eager to get on her way. She climbed into the cart and grabbed the reins, snapping them and guiding Flame back onto the road.

Chapter Eight

There weren't many people about, either buggies or cars. Mary sat stiffly on the bench, feeling the cold seep into her. She suddenly felt very tired, which was a puzzle as ironing wasn't a particularly strenuous chore. She decided she was simply worn down with all the tension between her and Mark.

Something had to be done.

The grooves at the side of the road were deep, and she barely had to guide Flame. She let her mind wander, trying to concentrate on the stark beauty of the nearly-naked trees. She didn't notice the buggy behind her until it was practically on top of her.

Flame skittered slightly, and a loud, "Whoa!" sounded from behind.

Mary gasped, her fingers curling tighter on the reins. Her eyes stretched wide, and the cold air dried them instantly. She blinked but didn't turn around. Indeed, she couldn't move. She heard the buggy behind her leave the well-worn grooves on the road and come closer, rolling up to her left. Still, she didn't move. Her gaze was frozen forward, her fingers now cramping from the strain of clenching the reins.

"Maria!" came his voice. "Pull over!"

Warning flags blasted through her mind. Every instinct in her told her to keep going. Ignore him. Pretend she was deaf.

She needed to flee. Escape.

Now.

She sucked in a huge breath and glanced to her right. There was an empty patch of land, easily big enough to accommodate both their vehicles. It was rimmed with a row of trees, just enough to ensure some privacy.

Against her own will and better judgment, Mary's hands jerked the reins to the right, and Flame obeyed, pulling the cart to the middle of the patch. The horse stopped, and she dropped the reins in her lap. She was breathing heavily now, still afraid to look over at him.

His buggy pulled up to her left, and she heard the door open. Within seconds, he was standing beside her cart.

"Maria. I've been hoping to see you."

Her breath scraped up her dry throat, and her stomach lurched with sudden nausea. She was going to vomit again. She could feel it. She closed her eyes and concentrated hard on remaining still. She placed her hands on her stomach, willing it to settle.

"Maria?" His voice was close and low and resonant.

She couldn't hold back any longer. She turned and gazed at him.

"Ike," she choked out.

His face opened up into a huge smile. "*Ach*, Maria. It's amazing to see you again." He reached out and brushed two fingers down her cheek.

She flinched, feeling the burning trail his fingers left

on her skin. Her hand flew to her cheek as if she could rub it away.

He frowned slightly. "Are you all right?" His eyes traveled over her, landing again on her face. "You look so beautiful. Just as I remembered."

"Remembered?" she asked, her voice barely functioning.

"Of course. I remember everything about you. Your gorgeous brown eyes and the way they crinkle when you're about to laugh. Your silky hair, although I wish I could see it hanging loose, down to your waist. Your sense of play—"

"Stop!" she cried. "Stop! I'm married."

His hands dropped to his sides, and he regarded her calmly. His eyes didn't leave hers. Finally, she looked away. She couldn't stand to see the familiarity of him. She couldn't bear having him so close.

"Don't you remember me at all?" he whispered, stepping even closer to her.

Her eyes flew up. "Remember you?" She couldn't believe what she was hearing. *"Remember you?"*

Her voice climbed in pitch until she was nearly shouting. Her face went hot, and she clapped her hand over her mouth.

"Maria… It's me. Ike."

She gaped at him, her eyes so wide, they burned. "I know who you are."

He smiled again. "I've been so eager to see you. I couldn't believe my luck when I saw you in the cart right there in front of me."

She looked at his easy grin and wanted to slap him. "It's been nearly four years now, Ike. *Four years*."

"I know. It's astounding how quickly time passes."

Her mouth dropped open, and she shook her head. "Is that *all* you have to say? How quickly time passes?" She scooted across the seat and grabbed his arm. "It didn't pass so quickly for me."

He stepped back from her intensity. "Maria! Are you mad at me?"

"Are you *insane*?" she countered.

"But…but, why? I thought you'd be happy to see me." Was he *lame in the brain*?

She wanted to cry out against the indignity of it all. For in truth, she *was* happy to see him. *Happy?* No, that wasn't the right word. But *something*. Having him near her again, so close that she could even catch his scent… So close that she could see every expression in his eyes? So close that…

She shuddered. And what did that make her? A wretched, disloyal wife, that was what. She cringed and fought the hot tears burning behind her eyes.

"Four years ago, I would have been happy to see you again. *Three* years ago. *Two years*. Even *one* year ago, I would have been happy." She snatched up the reins she'd dropped and was ready to snap them and get Flame back on the road.

But Isaac grabbed her hands in his large one and held on. She had no choice but to stop. She looked at him again.

"Let go of me," she said calmly, enunciating every word. "Let go of me."

"I won't. Not yet." He swung up into the cart and sat next to her. "I'm sorry, Maria. I'm so sorry."

His scent. The soap, the shampoo he used, the way the cool autumn air clung to his coat. A huge trembling shook through her, and she began to cry.

"*Ach*, Maria." He reached out and pulled her to him. "I'm sorry."

For a split second, she let herself melt into him. And then, in horror, she stiffened and drew away. "I'm married," she told him again.

"You didn't wait for me." It wasn't a question.

"I… I didn't—" And then she slapped him. Hard. Across the face. Horrified beyond belief, she gasped and covered her mouth. She'd hit him. *Hit* him! Who ever heard of such a thing? Mortified, she buried her face in her hands.

He gently peeled her hands away from her face. He held them, rubbing his thumbs over them in circles. "It's all right, Maria. I deserved that, I suppose."

She looked at him through her tears. "You…suppose?"

He gave her a gentle smile. A familiar smile. An intimate smile. She remembered how she had loved his smile. Loved the way his lips went up a bit higher on the left side than the right.

He shook his head. "*Nee*. I *know* I deserved that. I've hurt you, and I'm sorry."

She felt suddenly weak, as if she would collapse onto the floor of the cart just as if she had no bones to hold her up. He must have noticed because he let go of her hands and put his arm around her waist, supporting her.

"I never intended to be gone so long." He frowned. "I'm sorry I hurt you. I never intended to."

"But, you did," she whispered.

"I see that. I'm sorry." His eyes misted over, and for a second, she thought he'd join her in crying. But just as quickly, his tears were gone. "So. You've married."

"*Jah*."

"I knew that, of course. Mark Schrock."

"*Jah.*"

"Lucky man."

She wanted to wail out how wrong he was. Mark Schrock was *not* a lucky man.

Isaac tenderly tucked a strand of hair behind her ear. "Are you happy, Maria?"

She stared at him and didn't answer.

"*Ach*, Maria. I'm so sorry." He took a deep breath. "If it helps, I did miss you. Terribly."

Tears dripped down her face. "I missed…you…." She paused. She couldn't be having this conversation. It was wrong. Deep, down to her very soul, wrong.

"I need to go," she blurted.

He stiffened and backed away. "*Jah.* It would be best."

Their eyes locked. Neither of them moved. Mary nearly choked on the emotion blazing between them.

She swallowed. "Please, get down. I have to go."

He moved slowly, climbing out of the cart, but keeping his eyes on her. "Will we… Can we visit more sometime? I'd like to know everything that happened while I—"

"*Nee*," she snapped. "*Nee*. We can't. Good-bye, Ike."

She yanked the reins to the right, circling the small patch of land to get back out onto the road. When she rolled onto the asphalt, she snapped the reins again, knowing Flame would take her home.

Chapter Nine

Mary sat on the davenport in her front room, staring off into space. Her mind kept circling around her encounter with Ike. He looked good. The same, more or less. Oh, there were a few signs that he was older, but not much. His easy smile still had the power to entrance her.

Guilt crept up her spine. Had she sinned by talking to him? Surely, not. Surely, exchanging a few sentences wasn't a sin.

But the guilt assailed her, twisting her stomach In a knot. She had to be careful. She didn't want to vomit again.

She stood and stumbled across the room to the window. She clutched the cotton curtains and pressed her face against the glass. The cool surface was calming, and she breathed deeply.

The problem was that now she had more questions than she'd had before. Not knowing why Isaac had stopped writing to her had tormented her for years. She'd always thought that if she could only speak to him, ask him what had happened, hear his voice again, she would be healed of her pain. But now, she knew that wasn't true. She'd gained no real knowledge from their interchange.

Only that he'd missed her. She let go of the curtains and pressed her hands against her chest. She shook her head and blinked back the tears. If he'd truly missed her, he would have kept writing.

Oh, she was a fool.

Yet she wanted to talk to him again. She did. One more time. She wanted to ask him point blank why he'd ignored her. Why he thought she'd possibly be glad to see him after all these years.

Maybe, *he* was the fool.

What had he been doing all that time? She'd heard snippets here and there. He'd gotten some kind of job. But that was all she'd heard. Nothing more. She knew that he must have made a whole new circle of friends. He loved people. There was no way he would have stayed away unless he'd made very close friends.

And there had to have been a girl.

She inhaled sharply. She'd known that for years. Why else would he have left her?

She glanced at the kitchen clock. She needed to get supper ready. Mark could be home soon; although, she kind of doubted it. It was a long trip up north to the auction. But still, she should have something ready just in case.

She walked to the refrigerator and looked inside. There was some left-over meatloaf and a bowl of mashed potatoes. She could heat them up. A half loaf of bread was on the counter. She could slice that, too.

Mary supposed that she should eat something any-way, whether Mark showed up in time for supper or not. She hadn't been eating much, and she knew she was losing weight.

She heard the crunch of gravel and stepped to the kitchen window. A white van was pulling into the drive. *Mark.* So, he was home. She snatched the dishtowel and wiped her face. Then she smoothed her hair under her *kapp*.

Straightening her shoulders, she went to the front door and opened it. Mark was climbing out of the van, bidding the driver farewell. He turned to her.

"Hello, Mary."

"You're back then," she said, holding the door open a little wider.

He nodded and took the steps up the porch two at a time. "I'm back."

She craned around him. "Don't see any new horse."

He glanced at her, as if trying to discern whether she was joking or not. He smiled. "*Nee.* You don't see a new horse."

"Come on in. I'm getting supper ready," she said.

They went inside, and Mary closed the door behind them. "Guess who's back in Hollybrook?" she blurted. Her breath caught. She hadn't intended to tell him so quickly. She chewed her lip. Maybe, he hadn't heard her.

He gazed at her, one eyebrow cocked. "Who?"

She swallowed and blew out her breath. It was too late to back out of it now. "Isaac Studer." She said his name quickly and then bustled by Mark, busying herself with the supper preparations.

The only noise was the clanking of dishes as she placed the food into a skillet for a quick warm-up. She was afraid to look at Mark, so she kept her eyes on her task.

"How do you know?" He was right behind her. She could feel his breath on the back of her neck.

"I… I saw him," she uttered.

He took her arm and turned her around. Apprehension coursed through her, and she stared at him. Emotions flickered across his face, too quickly for her to read them.

"Where? Where did you see him?" he finally asked.

"I saw him when I was returning from Deborah's." She took a tight breath, wishing she'd kept her mouth quiet. The least she could have done was waited until he had something in his stomach.

"Deborah's?"

"*Jah*. She and I had a nice visit. I helped with her ironing."

"Her ironing…?"

She could see that his mind was not on the ironing. "She's in the family way, you know. She's mighty tired these days."

"I see." He let go of her. "So, Isaac passed you on the road?"

Her heart slammed against her ribs. "*Nee*. He stopped to visit when he saw me driving the cart."

Mark's eyes darkened. "Did he now?"

"*Jah*. Just for a minute."

"And what did he have to say?"

"Not much." She blinked up at him, working to keep her voice neutral.

"I see."

She licked her lips. "Are you hungry? This won't take me but a minute."

He took a step back. "Hungry…?"

"*Jah*. Meat loaf and potatoes. And I thought to cut

some bread. Will that be enough?" She turned and finished laying the slices of meat loaf into the skillet. She scooped out the potatoes and flattened them into patties.

Mark didn't answer her. He walked out of the kitchen and into the wash room. She heard him turn on the faucet to wash his hands.

She was shaking now. The spatula trembled in her fingers as she poked at the food. She heard the low sizzle as the burner grew hot beneath the pan. She listened intently for further sounds from the wash room. It had gone silent. What was he doing in there? Just standing? Waiting? And for what?

Her chest hurt. Why did Isaac have to come back anyway? Their conversation hadn't gone far enough for her to find out anything. Part of her now regretted leaving so quickly. She didn't know anything more than before. All the questions that had choked her for years weren't answered.

She had half a notion to run out of the house and hitch Flame up again. She froze.

And do what?

Drive the cart over to the Studers' farm? Knock on the door and ask if Isaac could come out to play? She was losing her mind. Even when they were courting, she wouldn't have dared go to his house. And now? As a married woman?

She grabbed the edge of the stove, leaning over and breathing hard. The steam from the skillet rose and swirled around her face.

"Mary?"

His voice was low and thick and pinched. She blew out her breath and straightened. She turned to him.

"*Jah*?" She tried, oh how she tried to put on a pleasant, innocent face. But when she saw his expression harden and the anger in his eyes, she knew she'd failed. Miserably failed.

"I'm not hungry," he stated. He marched across the room and out the door.

No. Not again.

Mary flipped the burner off and ran after him. The cold air outside felt good as it hit against her face. Mark was already halfway to the barn. She raced after him.

"Mark!" she called. "Stop! Wait!"

But he didn't stop. He walked into the barn, and she hurried in after him. It took a moment for her eyes to adjust to the shadows. She scanned the area and saw him standing next to the plow.

"Mark?" She slowed now, approaching him with hesitation.

His back was to her. She walked close and pressed herself against his back. She felt him stiffen even as she put her arms around him.

"Don't be mad," she whispered. "Please."

He plucked her arms from his waist and turned to face her. "Mad? That's what you think this is?"

She blinked and stepped back. "Isn't it?"

He shook his head and stared at her as if she'd gone crazy. "You think I'm mad?"

"Well, aren't you?"

He gazed upward and let his breath seep out in a hiss. "Maybe, I am. *Jah.* Maybe, I am."

"Don't be."

He laughed then, a rueful sound that echoed throughout the barn. "*Don't be.* Just like that? *Don't be mad.*"

She frowned, her forehead creasing into a mass of

furrows. She opened her mouth to speak but then realized she had no idea what to say.

He leaned down, his face level with hers. "Was it *gut* to see him? Were you happy?"

She winced and took another step back. "I... I..."

"I imagine you were thrilled. *Isaac Studer has come home.*" The bitter words dripped from his tongue.

She bit down on her lip to keep it from trembling. She couldn't cry. Not now. She just couldn't. She stared at him, her eyes stinging with unshed tears.

And then he folded in on himself. His shoulders slumped, and he seemed to shrink before her eyes. "*Ach,* Mary. I'm sorry." He held both of her shoulders. "I'm so sorry."

He leaned forward until his forehead touched hers. "Forgive me. Please."

Her throat tightened, and she fought her tears. "It's all right," she eked out.

She closed her eyes and sent up a prayer.

Mark straightened and wiped his face. He inhaled deeply. "Shall we go eat?" he asked.

"*Jah. Jah,*" she answered.

He put his arm around her, and the two of them walked back to the farmhouse together, she leaning ever-so-lightly against his side.

That night, Mary waited for Mark to come to bed. She'd put an extra quilt on the bed, wanting it to be snuggly warm. She'd brushed her hair an extra-long time and made sure that she wore her freshly laundered gown. She slipped under the covers and listened for his approach. He was banking the fire in the warming stove downstairs, and she expected him up at any moment.

But the minutes ticked by, and she didn't hear him. Her breathing became jagged as she once again fought her tears. Surely, he would come up any minute now.

She went back over everything that had been said between them that evening. She didn't know what else she could have done. Except not have told him about Isaac's return at all. But that wouldn't have been right. She had to tell him they'd spoken.

What if someone had seen them there, in that clearing?

She pressed her hand to her throat. Was that why she'd told Mark? Only because someone might have seen her with Isaac?

No. No. She'd told Mark because it was the right thing to do.

She heard a creak on the stairs. He was coming. Finally. He was coming. She lay still, staring at the ceiling where the flickering lantern tossed its light. He entered the room, and her gaze went to him. He wasn't looking at her. He shrugged out of his clothes, hanging them on the waiting pegs. He draped his suspenders on top of his shirt.

She watched him move. Watched his taut, strong arms pull on his nightclothes. Watched the curve of his back, the set of his shoulders. He turned around.

Their eyes met, and for a long moment, he didn't move. And then he sighed and came to the bed. "It's going to be a long day tomorrow," he said, blowing out the lantern.

He got into bed and pulled the covers high. He turned on his side, away from her, and said nothing more.

A long day tomorrow? She had no idea what that

meant. But she could read his body language clearly enough. She flopped onto her side, away from him.

She waited a long time for sleep to come.

Chapter Ten

"You need to see Old Mae," Deborah told her.

Mary grimaced. "Don't like to waste the woman's time."

Deborah snorted and poured a bit more tea into their mugs. "What do you mean, waste her time? That's what she does. She takes care of us all. You could see if she has any herbs for your nausea, but I think you and I both know what's going to cure it."

Mary looked at her.

"Nine months." Deborah put her hand on Mary's arm. "Or more like eight, I'm thinking."

Mary's jaw clenched. She'd purposely been avoiding what had been staring her right in the face for weeks. She didn't need Old Mae to tell her she was pregnant. She already knew.

"More like seven and a half, I'm thinking." Mary thought back to that night with Mark. With some quick ciphering in her head, she figured that had been about eight or nine weeks ago.

"So, you've known."

"*Jah*. But I didn't want to face it."

Deborah sat back in her chair and rested her hands on her own hugely protruding belly. "Why ever not? It's the best news ever. Does Mark suspect?"

Mary rubbed her forehead. "*Nee*. We don't talk much."

"*Ach*, Mary. Is he still upset? Isaac Studer's been back for months now."

"Not months. Maybe five weeks or so."

"Still…"

Abruptly, Mary got up from the table and began pacing a circle around Deborah's kitchen. "I know. I've tried."

"Have you?"

Mary flashed her a look of irritation. "Of course, I have. But there's this wall between us now. I can't… Well, I can't seem to get through it."

"You just have to reassure Mark. Show him how much you love him."

Mary stared at her best friend. She made it sound so simple. But, it wasn't. It wasn't simple at all. Mark would hardly look at her these days. He spent every spare minute at someone else's place, helping with whatever. It didn't seem to matter what it was—anything, just so he wouldn't have to remain at home.

With her.

"I've tried," she said again weakly, her voice fading.

Deborah hauled her heavy frame from her chair and moved close. "But now…" She smiled at Mary. "Now, you have this wonderful news to share. He'll be thrilled."

"Will he?" Mary seriously doubted it.

"Of course, he will. *Ach*, Mary, you mustn't waste

any time in telling him." She patted Mary's arm. "You'll see. He'll be so excited that everything will change. *Everything.*"

Mary's eyes misted over. "I hope so. Truly, I do."

A wail sounded from upstairs. Deborah laughed. "That will be Ross." She laughed again. "He hasn't much patience when he first wakes up from his nap."

"Do you want me to get him for you?"

"*Nee.* I enjoy getting him up." She shook her head. "If only climbing the stairs wasn't such a bother."

Mary nodded. "Not for much longer."

"*Nee.* Not for much longer. And I'm ready, let me tell you." She rubbed her stomach. "Then, it will be your turn to grow as big as your barn."

Mary forced a laugh. "I need to be going now. Bye, Deborah."

Deborah was already halfway to the stairs. She paused and turned back. "Tell him, Mary. *Soon.*"

"*Jah.* I will."

Mary bundled up in her cape, fastening it beneath her chin. She wound a knitted scarf around her neck and pulled on her mittens. Then she went outside and hurried down the steps to her pony cart. She climbed in and directed Flame out to the road.

The air was cold but still. There wasn't even the faintest breeze as Mary started down the road. The movement of the cart brushed the cold across her face, but she wasn't going at any great speed. Flame clip-clopped his way down the side of the road as if he had all day.

And then, she saw him… Ahead of her, not more

than a hundred yards. Walking. Even all bundled up, she knew it was him. But then, she would recognize him anywhere. She pulled up on the reins, not knowing what to do.

There was no other way to her house. Of course, she could circle around and go the long way home, but that would add a good hour to her trip. She bit the corner of her lip, deliberating. She supposed she could simply drive on by and not acknowledge him. Her heart pounded, and she felt a hint of perspiration on her upper lip.

This was ridiculous. She was a grown woman. She could drive her cart past an old friend without having heart failure. Resolutely, she snapped the reins and continued on her way. When she was closing in on him, he must have heard her cart because he swirled around with a big grin on his face.

When he saw who it was, his grin faltered, but only for the briefest second. Then it was back, and he raised his arm in greeting.

"Maria," he cried, and she couldn't ignore the pleasure in his tone.

She snapped the reins again and made to go by him with only a brief nod, but as she neared, he reached out and grabbed Flame's halter. The horse came to a jolting stop.

"How nice to see you," Isaac said. His face was flushed with the cold, but his gaze on her was warm and familiar.

"I'm in a hurry, Ike," she told him.

"Not in too much of a hurry to chat with an old friend. Surely."

Mary tugged on the reins. "I really am in a hurry."

He didn't respond but only looked at her. She stared into his eyes and saw that he knew full well she was lying.

Chapter Eleven

"Mark doesn't want you talking to me," Isaac stated.

Mary felt her cheeks go red. Did he have to be so frank? Was this something he learned in the *Englisch* world?

"*Nee*," she answered so softly, she could hardly hear herself.

"I get that." He patted Flame on the neck and rubbed him between his ears. And then he went still. "How long did you wait for me?" he finally spoke again, not looking at her.

She hesitated and then told him. "Three years."

She saw him flinch, and then he looked over at her. "Three *years*?"

"Until Mark told me that it was useless."

He recoiled. "*Ach*, Maria."

She squared her shoulders. "Mark was right. It was useless. I was being foolish."

His expression tightened. "It's my own fault," he said, turning more fully toward her. "Something I've grown to regret with every fiber of my being."

She tensed. He couldn't be saying such things to her. It was completely wrong. Completely inappropriate. She opened her mouth to tell him so, and then was overtaken by such a huge surge of resentment that her insides went hard. She seethed with anger, so overwhelming, so unexpected, that she stopped breathing.

"Maria?" He stepped closer, his face filled with concern.

She clenched her teeth, forcing air into her lungs, feeling her features contort.

"Maria?" he said again.

"How *dare* you!" she spat at him. "How dare you come back and upset everything! *Everything*, mind you! How dare you stop me on the road to talk to me! How dare you pretend that we can be friends! We can't be friends. *Ever.* Never, never, never in a million years!"

She was heaving with exertion. She was beside herself with her own vulnerability to him.

A sudden thick chill hung between them.

Her nostrils flared, and she glared at him with burning, reproachful eyes. A wave of nausea swept through her, and the edges of her vision clouded. She swayed, finding nothing to grasp. Within seconds, Isaac was in the cart with her, grabbing the reins and taking off down the road.

"Lean on me," he said tightly.

She had no choice. She was ready to flop right out of the cart.

"Breathe," he told her. "Breathe."

She was blacking out. She could feel herself slipping into unconsciousness. She felt a strong arm around her and everything went dark.

* * *

"Maria? Maria?"

Someone was slapping her face. Not hard. Really gentle-like. She felt woozy and didn't want to open her eyes.

"Maria?"

Wait. *Maria?* No one called her that. No one, except…

Her eyes flew open, and she stared up into Isaac's face. He was close, so close. Without thinking, she reached up and touched his lips.

A look of relief flooded his face. "*Ach.* You scared me half to death. Are you all right?"

She jerked her hand away from his mouth and looked around. "What happened? What are you doing here?"

She struggled to sit up and realized she was in the back of her pony cart. She scanned the area. "Where are we? Is this the same place we…?"

"*Jah.* Where we talked the other day. Maria, you fainted. Are you ill?"

She wanted to cry at him that no, she wasn't ill. She was pregnant. But Mark didn't even know that yet. She could hardly tell Isaac before telling her own husband.

She realized with shock that Isaac was holding her hand. She yanked it free and scooted back up against the side of the cart.

"I need to go. I need to go now."

"You're so angry with me."

She let out her breath in a long sigh. "It's gone now," she whispered.

"It'll be back."

She shrugged. "Maybe." But he was right, it would be back. How she wished she didn't care anymore. Hadn't she learned that such debilitating anger always indicated how much a person was still emotionally involved.

"I was completely bewitched," he said softly. He had been squatting beside her in the cart. Now, he eased himself down to sit cross-legged beside her.

She gaped at him. "Bewitched?"

"*Jah*. With everything in the *Englisch* world. After a few months, I was so heady with it all, I started to pretend I wasn't Amish." He gave a rueful laugh. "Of course, my accent gave me away. But then, I told people I was from Europe, and they bought it."

She stared at him.

"I did it all. Lived the full fancy life. Do you know that I have my driver's license? I'm a *gut* driver, too. I even enrolled in a few classes at a community college." His features grew animated. "It's fun to learn new things, Maria. It gets your blood going. Truly."

He sobered again. "I drank. Not too much. I never got careless. I went to movies, bars, night clubs. There's a whole world out there. I knew you would never, never, never approve, so it was just easier to stop writing."

He looked at her then, his eyes shadowed and his expression contrite. "I was a fool. I didn't even have the decency to let you know what was happening."

Her throat tightened, and she felt anger again fighting to surface. She pressed her hands to her stomach and forced herself to be calm.

"It was wrong, and I'm sorry. I thought… Well, I thought…" He blew out his breath and rubbed his hand over his jaw. "I don't know what I thought. That you'd wait for me? That you'd go on without me? I don't know. I was too busy thinking only of myself to think about you. Or us."

He took her hand again and rubbed it between his. "I'm sorry. I was cruel. And to think…" He choked up then, blinking rapidly and clearing his throat. "And to think that you waited for me for three years."

Mary bit her lip to keep it from quivering. With lightning speed, she'd gone from anger to pain, and neither of them gave her any relief.

"I worked. At a gas station. I had a roommate because I didn't make enough money to live on my own. My roommate…" He paused and seemed to be screwing up his courage. "My roommate…was a girl."

Mary sucked in air, feeling her throat tighten. *"What?"*

"Don't get the wrong idea. We weren't together. Not really. She was nice. And a good roommate. She wanted more… But, I guess…" He looked into her eyes. "I guess I hadn't completely forgotten you."

Mary blanched. She moved to get up, but he pulled her back down.

"Nee. Don't go. Not yet."

She glared at him. "Why are you telling me this? I don't want to hear about you living with a girl all those months that I was waiting for you. Biding my time. Certain that you'd come back to me. Certain that you still… loved me." She shook her head, incredulous. "Ike, what in the *world* were you thinking?"

"I wasn't thinking. Maria, I wasn't. But I came to my senses."

She gaped at him.

"I did! I'm back now. Truly back. For *gut.* Doesn't that prove it?"

She sat there, astounded and shaken to her very core. "But that has *nothing* to do with me. Not anymore."

She pried her hand loose and climbed over the bench,

snatching up the reins. He climbed over the bench to join her.

"Ike, you have to get out," she said.

"But, Maria…"

"I'm serious. Get out!"

He nodded. "You're right. I'm sorry. You're right. I'm getting out. Forgive me."

The lump in Mary's throat had grown to monstrous proportions. She could barely swallow.

"Please forgive me," he whispered and climbed out of the cart.

Their eyes locked.

"Please," he repeated. He turned away, raising his arm in farewell. She sat, unmoving, as he walked out of the clearing and back to the road.

She dropped the reins and put her arms around herself. *It's all right,* she thought, fighting her tears. *Everything is going to be all right. Just breathe. Just pray. Just go home to your husband. Go home, Mary. Go home. Go home.*

She picked the reins back up and guided Flame onto the road. But all the way home, her mind was filled with that last look Isaac had given her. That last desperate look. He still loved her. He'd been horrid to her. *Worse* than horrid.

But yes, he still loved her.

Chapter Twelve

Mary couldn't sit still. She'd cleaned everything so vigorously; her arms were aching. After rubbing every surface in the kitchen and the bathroom, she'd attacked the floors, sweeping and scrubbing and mopping and rinsing.

This burst, coming so soon after her last cleaning frenzy, meant that by midmorning, there was nothing left to clean. She sank down onto the davenport, exhausted. She took a huge gulping breath and knew that this was the day.

This was the day that she had to tell Mark. She pressed her hands against her stomach and wondered how he'd react. Surely, he'd be happy. *Surely.* Every man she knew was happy when his wife was in the family way.

She and Mark had been married long enough now. Not so long for people to wonder if there was a problem. Nor so short for people to wonder what they'd been up to before the ceremony. Mary leaned back and closed her eyes. She got weary of the gossip train sometimes, but she knew it was normal. In any community, people talked. That was just the way it was.

Her nausea was better these days. At least, she didn't feel sick all day long. It only came and went now. She'd even had a few days when she'd felt fine all day long. Physically, anyway. She wasn't passing any days when she didn't feel the sting of her situation with Mark.

She got up and walked to the window, peering outside. She couldn't see any sign of Mark. In truth, she didn't know what he did outside these days. She still harbored the secret fear that he was only out there to avoid her.

The days were moving quickly toward the holidays and winter, a time when Mark should have more occasion to spend the hours inside. With her.

She leaned her face against the pane of glass and felt the cool surface on her skin. She was still warm and sweaty from her cleaning binge and the cool touch felt good. Refreshing, almost. She glanced toward the kitchen. Even though summer had long gone, she should make some lemonade. She had at least four lemons in the bottom of the refrigerator.

Mark might like to have lemonade with the noon meal. She went into the kitchen and retrieved the lemons. She took the glass lemon juicer from the shelf and then cut the lemons in half. She set one of the halves onto the juicer and leaned in, squeezing the lemon back and forth. Tangy-smelling juice dribbled into the base.

The side door of the house opened and banged shut. Was Mark back? She glanced up at the clock. It was still well before noon. But by the shuffle of footsteps, she knew it was him.

She looked toward the wash room door. "Mark? That you?"

He came into the kitchen. "Don't know who else it would be," he said. "You expectin' someone else?"

"*Nee*," she said quickly. "I'm making lemonade."

His brows rose at that. "Hmm."

"I know it's not the season, but I thought you might enjoy some."

He didn't answer her, but he did give her an extra-long gaze before walking to the fridge and opening it. "I'm hungry. Don't rightly know why. We ate breakfast."

"We can eat the noon meal early if you like."

"*Jah*. If you don't mind." He shut the fridge and then seemed to feel out of place. He wandered to the doorway, stopped, looked around as if trying to find something, and then with a sigh, he started toward the front room.

"Mark?"

He paused.

"Can we talk about something this afternoon?"

She saw him tense.

"This afternoon?"

"*Jah*. After the noon meal." She wasn't going to be so foolish as to discuss something of import on an empty stomach again.

"*Nee*…" He dragged the word out, and her eyes widened. He wouldn't even talk to her anymore?

But she had misunderstood his intention.

"Let's talk now," he said curtly. He went straight into the front room to sit down.

"But—" she started to protest, but he was already gone. She followed him to the front room and sat beside him, which seemed to surprise him.

He stiffened and scooted over an inch or two, giving her ample space.

"What is it?" he asked.

She blinked. This was *not* how she'd planned to tell him. She opened her mouth and then shut it again. She wanted to tell him happier. Better. Not like this.

"Well?"

She licked her lips. "I just had something I wanted to tell you."

"So you said."

"It's, well…" She took in a huge breath. "It's important."

"I reckoned."

"I went to see Deborah the other day."

"I know." He frowned at her. "Come, Mary. What is this about?"

"I'm in the family way," she blurted. She kept her eyes glued to his face, wanting to see how he would take the news but also fearing his reaction.

At first, he didn't respond. Then, she saw his jaw flex slightly. He sucked in a long slow breath. She could see the wheels in his head turning—speculating, figuring. She knew what he was doing. They hadn't been intimate for some time. In fact, for a long time. Except that once.

"When is the *boppli* due?" he asked stiffly, a look of dread on his face.

So…

That was it, then?

He was trying to figure out if it was his. She knew him. She could see the doubt stamped all over his face. *Ach,* that he could *think* it was anyone's but *his.* A huge wave of grief pounded into her, battering her down until she couldn't breathe. She gasped and sputtered, struggling for air. Her eyes watered as she tried to take it in. The agony of his doubt ripped through her, twisting her insides until she couldn't remain still.

Had they really sunk to such depths?

Mary lurched to her feet, bolstering herself to a standing position by grabbing onto the arm of the davenport. She stood for a second, trembling so badly, she thought she might fall back down. But she didn't. With bile pooling at the sides of her mouth, she turned and ran from the room. She could barely see where she was going. Grabbing the stair rail, she yanked herself upward.

She had to get away. She couldn't be in the same room as him. She couldn't *look at him*.

A gulping sob broke loose from her throat. She thrust through her bedroom door and threw herself on the bed—her heart wailing. She covered her face with her hands and felt the bitter tears pour through her fingers.

Chapter Thirteen

Mary had no idea how long she'd lain there. She must have fallen asleep, which was shocking considering how upset she'd been. She felt chilled, and the room was steeped in shadows. What time *was* it? She stirred, sitting up and rubbing her eyes. It had to be late afternoon. She could see the sky through the naked branches outside. The gray clouds were thick, covering the sky like heavy syrup. It looked to be close to six o'clock, but that couldn't be right. She couldn't have slept that long.

She glanced at the wind-up clock on the bedside table. It was barely four o'clock. Even so, that meant she'd slept for hours. She got up, feeling a bit woozy. Where was Mark? Had he left?

A bitter metallic taste filled her mouth. She ran her tongue over her teeth and tried to swallow the taste away. It wouldn't leave.

She listened and heard nothing. The house was completely still. Mark must have left, all right. But where would he have gone? And why hadn't he come up to talk with her? She sucked in a long breath.

Maybe, he didn't love her anymore. Or maybe, he was just plain sick of her.

Why, oh why, did Isaac have to come back? He hadn't even told her his reasons. But as she lamented it, she knew Isaac's return wasn't the whole problem. She and Mark were having difficulties before Isaac returned. She and Mark had been having difficulties since the first week of their marriage.

It was her fault. She knew it was.

Even as she'd let Mark talk her into giving up all hope of Isaac, she'd continued to harbor a small corner of expectation. As if Isaac might still return for her. Come back to her. Prove his love for her.

In truth, she was fond of Mark. She supposed she even loved him. But he'd had no chance. How could he possibly compete with Isaac's memory? How could he possibly capture all her heart when most of it still rested squarely in Isaac's hand?

Oh, it was her fault all right.

She'd tried. But she couldn't simply turn love off, now, could she? She *wished* she could. She'd even prayed to have her love for Isaac taken away.

But it remained. Stubbornly stuck inside of her, with roots so deep and tangled, she couldn't find any way out.

She walked to the dresser and picked up the hand mirror. She turned it over and looked at her face in the shadows. Her brown eyes looked almost black, and they were sunken and hollow. Her mouth drooped, and she saw the sadness there. Months of sadness written there. A few strands of hair had come loose, and her *kapp* was askew.

She put down the mirror and took off her *kapp*. She unfastened her hair and let it fall in long curls down her back. She took her brush with her to the bed and sat down. She pulled the brush through her hair, feeling the tension in her scalp give way to the strokes.

The rhythm of her arm running down the length of her hair was mesmerizing, and she relaxed into it. When her hair began to cackle and cling to her arm, she dropped the brush in her lap.

Where was Mark? She wanted to see him. She wanted to somehow connect with him. She was having his child. She was his wife. He was her husband. They *had* to connect somehow.

And she had to discard Isaac once and for all...

She blinked back her tears, and without bothering to put her *kapp* back on, she went downstairs. She stepped lightly, as if afraid to disturb the air. Her hair swayed gently down her back and over her arms as her fingers whispered down the railing. When she stepped off the last step, she looked about, unsure of what to do.

Find Mark. That's what she had to do. *Find Mark.*

First, she needed to locate her shoes. Had she put them in the wash room? She had no recollection. She headed toward the room to check, when Mark's voice stopped her.

"Mary?"

She turned slowly to see him sitting in the semi-darkness on the davenport. Had he not moved since she'd left? Had he been sitting there *all this time*? For *hours*? Without thinking, she went to him and knelt before him.

His face and eyes were swollen, and he wore a haunted look. With a soft cry, she put her arms around him.

"*Ach*, Mark. I didn't know where you were."

He buried his face in her neck. He was shaking, and she realized he was crying. She tightened her grip on him.

"Mark," she whispered. "Mark."

She held him for a long time. When he drew away, his face was smeared with tears. "What has happened to us?" he asked, his voice low and scratchy.

Her throat squeezed nearly shut. She gulped, sucking in air.

"Sit with me." He pulled her up from the floor, and she sat beside him. "I'm sorry."

She let out a soft gasp.

He continued, "I'm so sorry. I don't know where my head was."

She leaned on his arm and rested her head on his shoulder. "It's my fault," she uttered. "Everything. All of it. It's my fault."

"*Nee*." He moved back, forcing her to sit up straight. He looked at her. "It's *my* fault. I shouldn't have pressured you. I shouldn't have forced you to marry me."

Her forehead creased. "You didn't force me." In a way, he had, but she'd allowed it to happen.

"*Jah*, I did." He reached up and ran his rough, work-worn hand over her long hair. He lifted a lock of it and fingered it gingerly. "You have beautiful hair, Mary."

She blinked.

"Beautiful, beautiful hair." His voice broke, and he took a minute to get himself back under control. "I'm sorry. For earlier."

"I know."

"I went insane there for a minute." He blew out his breath, and she nearly wept for the pain she saw on his face. "I am happy. About the *boppli* I mean. I want you to know that."

She put her fingers to her mouth. "*Gut*," she whispered. "I'm glad you're happy."

"It's wonderful *gut* news." He gazed at her, and the hurt and longing lay naked in his eyes.

"I'm happy, too," she uttered. She drew in a shaky breath and wondered if it was true. She closed her eyes for a moment and breathed. Yes. She was happy. She had a tiny life inside of her.

Yes. Yes. Of *course*, she was happy.

Now, this whole mess...this whole *everything*, wasn't just about her and Mark. Or even Isaac. It was about the baby.

She felt a strange tingling inside her and parted her lips in gratitude. It felt good. Good to put her mind somewhere else. To have a reason to stop dwelling on everything wrong. To stop moaning over her long-lost love.

Her breath caught, and she pressed her hands over her heart. Shame swept through her. What in the world had she been thinking? Why had she centered her life around what she thought she'd lost? She wanted to open her mouth and wail over her own selfishness.

To think of what she'd done. All these months. All these *years*.

She put a hand on Mark's knee. "I'm sorry, Mark. Truly."

He stared at her hand. "I know." He hesitated, his eyes on hers, dark and unfathomable. He inhaled. "I'll do my best to be a *gut* father to the child."

"Of course," she said quickly. "Of course, you will."

To the child? Not, to *our* child? His words sounded so cold.

"You're hungry," he said, not asking.

She nodded and started to stand.

"*Nee.* You stay here. I can get something put together." He stood up and without looking back at her, left the room.

She stared after him and then got up and lit the two lanterns in the room.

It was getting dark so early these days.

Chapter Fourteen

The next week passed in tenuous peace. Mary was on edge, striving to make everything tidy and comfortable and perfect for Mark. She ensured that the meals were hearty and on time. She did the laundry, though with her failing energy level, it took longer than normal. She harvested the last of the squash and stored them in the cellar. She even decided to repaint the outside of the front door that had started to peel.

But Mark stopped her, taking the brush from her hand and finishing it up himself.

There wasn't much talk between them, but Mary hoped that the tension had lessened. She thought it had, until Mark started to disappear again for longer and longer periods of time. From what she could tell, he still took refuge in the barn, but she wasn't about to go and check. She figured that would not only make her a pathetic wife, but it would annoy him. Who wanted someone following them around and spying on them?

By Wednesday of the following week, Mary needed to get out. She asked Mark to hitch up Flame, and she took the pony cart to see Deborah.

"You're here!" Deborah cried, coming out onto the porch to greet her. "Leave your horse. Eli will see to him."

Mary climbed down and went inside with her friend.

"Look at me," Deborah lamented, rubbing her huge stomach. "I'm about ready to explode."

Mary laughed. "I'll be looking that way soon enough."

"You been to see Old Mae yet?"

"*Nee.* But I'll go soon. I promise."

"And Mark? Does he know?"

Mary nodded.

"And?"

Mary winced. She couldn't possibly tell Deborah that Mark had doubted her fidelity. It wouldn't be right to reveal such a thing, and it wouldn't be fair to Mark.

"He's happy."

"You don't sound convinced." Deborah lay a hand on Mary's arm.

"*Nee*, really. He is. He's happy."

Deborah studied her for a long minute. "Tell me the truth."

Mary wilted. "All right. It was hard at first. But now, things are better. They *are*."

Deborah continued to regard her as if trying to dig for more behind her expression. "It's not me you have to convince."

"I know."

"It's still bad?"

"I thought it was better. But now, he's spending a lot of time away from me."

"What do you mean?"

"It's going on winter, Deborah. There isn't that much to do in the barn."

Deborah flicked her hand. "*Ach*, men. They'll always find something to do out in the barn."

Mary gave her a tremulous smile. "I suppose."

"Things will continue to improve. They will."

Mary nodded and looked down at her tummy. "I can hardly believe it," she whispered.

"It's always that way with the first one. I didn't believe it until Ross starting kicking me."

Mary chuckled. "I'm looking forward to feeling our *boppli's* kicks."

Deborah groaned. "Just you wait. It gets downright painful at times."

"I won't mind."

The two friends chatted for an hour. When Mary left, she felt much better. A sense of excitement about the future tugged at her heart for the first time in a very long time. It was such an unexpected feeling, that Mary felt almost giddy.

And she only wanted to do one thing—go home and tell Mark about it. She wondered at that. Didn't such a desire alone indicate that things were better? She blew out her breath. She was sick to death of analyzing everything. Couldn't she just go with her feelings and enjoy the fact that she wanted to see Mark? Wanted to talk to him?

As she neared their farm, she couldn't help herself… She slowed Flame down. She was nervous. If she rushed to tell Mark about her excitement, what if he spurned her?

Or worse, what if he did nothing? Didn't react at all.

Her chest constricted, and her grip on the reins tightened. She shook her head. No, she was borrowing trouble. Plain and simple. Hadn't her mother warned her against that time and time again as she was growing up?

But still, Flame moved slower and slower until he was barely walking forward down the road. When they reached the drive, Mary braced herself and turned in. She drove the cart straight to the barn.

Mark would probably be out there anyway.

She pulled up on the reins and climbed down. She went to the open barn door and peered inside. It appeared empty. She glanced back at the house but didn't see any movement there, either. She stepped farther into the barn.

"Mark?" she called. "You in here?"

There was a rustling noise from the loft and a few sprigs of hay fluttered down.

"Mark? You up there?"

What in the world was he doing in the loft? His head appeared over the edge, and he gave her a sheepish look.

"I didn't expect you back so soon," he told her.

"What are you doing up there?"

He sighed. "Nothing."

"Nothing?"

He gave her a shy smile, which was so surprising and so endearing, that she simply gaped at him.

"You weren't supposed to come home so soon."

She kept staring. Why not? What was he *doing* up there?

More rustling sounds and then he appeared at the ladder. "Come on up," he said.

Her eyebrows rose. "Up? You want me up there?"

He nodded.

Wondering what was so mysterious, she went to the ladder and carefully clung to the rungs, inching her way up. When she got to the top, she crawled onto the floor and then stood. She glanced around. Bales of hay had been pushed to the sides, creating a work space in the middle. There, she noted a sawhorse, a variety of tools, lots of sawdust, and...

She gasped.

Right there in the middle of the loft stood the beautiful beginnings of a cradle. Her hand flew to her mouth. Mark watched her, his expression guarded.

"Mark!" she uttered. She hurried over to the cradle and knelt before it, running her hands over the smooth wood. It looked to be half done, and the workmanship vibrated with love and care.

"Mark," she said again, tears choking her.

"Do you like it?" he asked, his voice hesitant.

"Like it?" She turned to look up at him. "I love it. It's perfect."

His entire body seemed to exhale with relief. "Is it?"

She stood and faced him. "*Jah*. It's perfect." She felt the tears flowing down her cheeks, but she made no move to wipe them away. She couldn't move. She couldn't do anything but gaze at her husband.

The air between them shrank until Mary felt encased in a warm cocoon. And then, as if on cue, they moved to each other, coming together in a tight embrace. Mary buried her face into his chest, and her tears wet his shirt. He smelled like hay and freshly cut wood and work.

Mark held her close and kissed the top of her head. "*Ach*, Mary. I'm so glad you like it."

She nodded and gulped, and her tears came faster.

He drew away only enough to look down into her eyes. "Please, don't fret. I know you've been fretting."

She swallowed past the lump in her throat and nodded at him.

And then together, they gazed down at the half-finished cradle. The light from the hanging lantern reflected off the shiny wood, encasing the two of them in its warm glow. Mary marveled at the beautiful cradle for the baby. *Their* baby.

She knew this didn't fix everything. She wasn't a fool. But it was a step, and she would gladly take any evidence that maybe, just maybe, things truly were getting better.

Chapter Fifteen

Mary pounded the masher up and down, leaving a few wayward lumps in the potatoes, just the way Mark liked them. She scooped them out, plopping the potatoes into a serving bowl and smiled. Ever since he'd shown her the cradle, things had been better between them. Not perfect by any stretch.

But better.

She looked down at her swelling belly, noting that she'd have to let out the seams of her dress again. She rubbed her hand over the bump. This baby was bringing them together. Just as she had prayed it would. She carried the potatoes to the table and set them next to the steaming platter of fried chicken. She glanced at the large clock over the window. Mark should be coming in any minute now.

The howling of the wind had picked up in the last hour. She shivered and went to the peg near the front door and took down her shawl, wrapping it around her shoulders. Through the window in the warming stove's door, she saw the fire was burning heartily, but there was still a chill in the air. The stack of wood next to the stove was dwindling. She'd have to ask Mark to replenish it.

She heard the side door in the wash room open, and a gust of wind blew through the house. Mark was back. He came in, balancing a heavy load of firewood in his arms. He leaned low and the chunks rolled down, thudding noisily into the wood box.

"Getting downright bitter out there," he said, straightening. He looked at the food-laden table. "I'll wash up and be back in a flick."

Mary hurried to pour the milk. Mark came back in and sat at the table.

"Smells right *gut*."

She slipped into the chair beside him. "I'm glad."

She watched him fold his work-roughened hands and bow his head. Wisps of blond hair hung about his face. He was due for a haircut soon. Perhaps after dinner, she would cut it for him. He closed his eyes, and she followed suit.

"Shall we thank the Lord *Gott*?" he asked.

They bowed for a few minutes of silent prayer, and then he cleared his throat, looking up and meeting her eyes. He smiled. It was genuine enough, not like the forced smiles of a few weeks or even months ago.

She returned his smile. A bit too polite, perhaps, but much better than the awkward gaping silences that had plagued their meals together. And Mark wasn't escaping out to the barn as often, either. Nowadays, he tended the animals and then came back inside.

"I see you left in some lumps," he said, around a mouthful of potatoes.

"That I did."

"Nice of you." He took another forkful.

She peeled the skin off her drumstick. Since she'd become pregnant, she could hardly abide any grease at all. It seemed to harden in her throat and sit in her stomach like a half-rotted stump.

Mark was watching her. "Still feeling sick?"

She frowned. "I'm not sick. I'm in the family way. There's a big difference."

He gave her a sheepish grin. "You're right. But, how are you feeling?"

"Fine." She took a small bite of chicken. It seemed to settle so she took another bite.

"I'll be helping at the Benders' tomorrow."

"Oh? What's going on?"

"The wind took down one of his trees and hit the side of his shed. Don't rightly know the extent of the damage, but we'll get it fixed right up."

"Will a lot of men be there? Shall I make some food and bring it over?"

Mark's brow creased. "Don't like you out in this weather."

"It's winter, Mark. I don't plan to stay cooped up the entire season."

He chuckled. "Still. I don't want you taking a chill."

"I'll bundle up."

He shrugged and helped himself to a thick slice of bread. "I'll think on it."

Mary regarded him, checking his expression to see if there was anything else there. A hidden concern. A doubt. A suspicion. She hated that she was checking, but she couldn't help herself.

Would Isaac Studer be at the Benders' tomorrow? Because if he was, Mark would not want her there.

Mary tried to discern whether Mark thought she

hoped Isaac would be there, so that she would have a chance to see him. And thus, her offer to bring food.

But Mark's expression appeared unruffled. Mary's mind whirled back to not so long ago. Mark's face had twisted with concern so often, it had become an ever-present grimace. His normal expression.

"Mary?"

She gave a start, realizing that he was looking at her. "Hmm?"

"What is it?"

His countenance had changed. It was tight. Hard. And just like that, once again Isaac Studer hung between them, so real, so tangible that he may as well have been sitting right there at the table. *Between them.* Mary's jaw tensed. What was *wrong* with her? Why had she been staring at Mark like that? Clearly, he had read her every thought as if she'd blazoned them across the ceiling with red paint.

"Nothing," she said quickly. "Would you like more chicken?"

She picked up the platter and offered it to him, but she was unable to meet his eyes. He didn't reach for any chicken, and she finally put the platter down again with a gentle clink.

The rest of the meal passed in silence.

Mark had taken to reading the Bible aloud every evening for thirty minutes or so. He'd told Mary that he wanted to get into the habit before their baby was born.

"My *dat* read to the family every night," he said. "I want to do the same."

That evening, he read the first few chapters of the book of Amos. Mary squirmed with discomfort as he droned on about the wicked shallowness of the people. The Prophet Amos warned them of their disobedience to God, and Mary couldn't help but wonder if Mark had chosen these particular passages with an ulterior motive.

She finally decided that he wouldn't be so heartless. He was likely reading Amos because the Bible had fallen open to that spot. At least, that was what she told herself. Besides, she had no cause for guilt. She'd done nothing wrong. Her conscience could be clear. She'd gone out of her way to tell Mark about her unexpected meeting with Isaac Studer. After all, when Isaac had come upon her on the road, it had been totally unplanned.

She sighed and sagged back in her rocker. But there were secrets. Or there had been. She'd tried to keep her love for Isaac to herself. She'd tried to smash it down, obliterate it.

Even God wouldn't have expected her to share something like that with her husband. Would he?

There was no answer. None. She sighed and continued to listen to Mark's voice.

Chapter Sixteen

Mary bundled herself up so tightly, she could barely move. The clothes constricted her movements so much that when she climbed into the pony cart, she felt like a very stiff, very old, and hardly mobile woman. She chuckled lightly as she picked up the reins. Before snapping them on Flame's rear-end, she checked her casserole. It was safely wedged against her left foot.

The Benders' farm was a good piece away, but Mary didn't mind. Even with the temperature hovering in the low forties, it was nice to get outdoors. Nice to feel the fresh, frosty air in her lungs. Nice to feel the sharp prickle of the cold on her face. It invigorated her, made her feel more alive.

"Come on, Flame," she said and clucked her tongue. "Let's get there in time to help serve the meal."

Flame moved, and the cart lurched forward. Within minutes, the horse was pulling her at a nice, steady pace, the wheels of the cart moving to a rhythm that was both relaxing and comforting. Mary huddled inside her heavy cape and let Flame take over, barely having to manage the reins.

It took a good thirty-five minutes to get to the Benders'. When Mary pulled onto their property, it was already buzzing with activity. She saw the men, gathered around a shed to the side of the barn next to a field. It looked like they were finishing up with the work. Some of them were already wandering back toward the barn, tools in their hands.

Mary counted seven buggies lined up in the yard. She caught sight of her best friend, Deborah, her new babe in arms and little Ross toddling beside her. They were headed to the big house. Mary stopped her cart and secured the reins. She picked up her chicken-noodle casserole, slipped out of the cart, and hurried to catch up with them.

"Deborah!" she called.

Deborah stopped and looked around. She smiled as Mary approached.

Mary drew close and peered beneath the quilt. "I can't believe you came out today. Is the *boppli* warm enough?"

"*Ach*, this girl is a tough one," Deborah said with pride.

Mary bent down to her little boy. "Hello, Ross. Nice to see you."

He stuck a mittened hand in his mouth and gazed at her with huge brown eyes.

"Let's get inside. My eyelashes are going to freeze to my face." Deborah laughed heartily. "Then my eyes will be plastered open forever."

Mary laughed. "It's *gut* to see you. I never dreamed you'd be here."

"Eli came to help the men, and I wasn't of a mind to stay home. I fear this winter is going to be a long, cold one."

"What does the *Farmer's Almanac* say?"

Deborah laughed again. "Goodness. I don't read that thing. I leave that to Eli."

Truth was, Mary didn't think Deborah had time to read anything what with the two young ones. They started into the house together, but Deborah paused on the porch.

"He's here," she whispered, giving Mary a meaningful look.

Mary's chest tightened with a wave of apprehension. She didn't need to ask Deborah whom she meant. She knew. Without thinking, she turned around, her eyes sweeping the group of men. And there he was. Walking into the barn. Mary could hardly mistake his ambling stride and the easy way his arms swung while he moved. All of his movements were smooth and buoyant, as if he harbored some amusing tidbit, something to laugh and be happy about.

"Mary," Deborah snapped under her breath. "Stop gawking."

But her warning came too late. At that precise moment, Mark and her father came out of the barn together, stepping aside to let Isaac pass. Mark's gaze flew to her, standing on the porch, staring. His head jerked to Isaac and then back to her.

Mary's father said something to Mark, and Mark took his eyes off her. But she'd seen it. The dawning on his face. The realization. He knew she'd been watching Isaac.

Her stomach twisted, and she felt ill.

"Come on," Deborah said. "Let's go inside."

Mary followed her inside to the large kitchen. The women were bustling about, getting the meal together.

Mary spotted her mother by the cook stove, stirring something in a large steaming pot. Mary hadn't seen her mother in over a week, and in that time, it seemed her mother had aged. Which, of course, was ridiculous.

But Mary was grateful to have something to take her mind off her own worries. She set her casserole on the table, and peeled off the thin quilt she'd wrapped it in. She noted that the dish was still fairly warm. She walked over to her mother.

"Hello, *Mamm*."

"*Ach*, Mary. *Gut* to see you, daughter." Mrs. Hochstetler studied Mary's face. "You're looking a bit tired. You getting the rest you need?"

"I'm doing fine, *Mamm*. Hardly any morning sickness at all now."

"You been to see Old Mae?"

"I saw her a couple of weeks ago. She gave me some tea and said I was doing real *gut*."

Her mother nodded. "The men are about finished out there, I think. We need to get all this on the table."

Mary glanced around. The other women were already setting everything on the table. In fact, a few extra folding tables had been added to the heavy wooden dining table, extending the eating area right into the front room.

Mary turned to help carry the food, but her mother grabbed her arm, stopping her.

"You sure you're all right," she asked in a low voice, close to Mary's ear.

Mary frowned and stepped back. "Of course, *Mamm*. I'm fine."

As soon as the words were spoken, a sharp pain shot up from her groin to her chest. She sucked in a surprised gasp and went completely still. But just as quickly, it was gone. She gave her mother a tremulous smile and moved away.

What *was* that? She'd never felt anything like it before. Well, it was gone now and that was all that mattered.

"Mary, can you take in the rest of the silverware?" Martha Bender asked her, holding out a handful of forks.

"*Jah.*" Mary took the utensils.

Within minutes, the men were stomping their boots in the wash room and cleaning up to eat. Mary scurried about with the rest of the women, finishing up the last of the preparations. The group was small enough for all of them to be seated together. The men sat at one table, and the women and children sat at the other two tables.

Ezekiel Bender led them in silent prayer during which Deborah struggled to keep little Ross quiet. Mary finally took the baby from Deborah and held her snugly against her shoulder. Mary nestled her head against the little girl's, breathing in her fresh baby smell. Soon, she was going to have her own child to snuggle with. It could hardly come soon enough. But right then, Mary was more excited for the day when she would feel the child move.

Just yesterday, she had thought she felt a little flutter inside, but it didn't last more than two seconds, so she'd dismissed it. Now, as she was hugging Rachel, she wondered if it had been her baby moving after all.

Ezekiel coughed slightly and everyone looked up. Martha picked up a platter of sliced cold cuts and started them around the table.

"Eat up, everyone," she said. "We've got ample."

Mary handed Rachel back to Deborah. As she did, her eye caught Mark's. She smiled, and he paused only an instant before smiling back. Mary glanced down at Rachel on her shoulder and back at him. Her smile widened. And for that moment, the fact that Isaac was sitting at the table with them faded into nothing. It was only she and Mark. Mark's expression grew tender, and she knew he was also thinking of the child growing within her.

The moment stretched, filling Mary with a deep new contentment, only interrupted when Deborah handed her a bowl of pickles.

"Your head in the clouds?" Deborah asked, chuckling.

"You might say so," Mary answered, dishing out a forkful of pickles onto her plate.

When everything was cleaned up, Mark joined Mary in the front room.

"Are you ready to go home?" he asked her.

"You won't be going with Josh?" Josh had given Mark a ride to the Benders early that morning.

"*Nee*. I'll take you home. We'll go together."

Mary smiled and brushed against his side. "I'd like that."

"Say your good-byes then, and I'll bring the cart around."

Mary pulled on her mittens and bid everyone farewell. By the time she got out onto the porch, Mark was pulling up with the cart. She stepped down and felt the same sharp pain as earlier. It zinged through her, taking her breath. She grabbed the railing, and it was gone. She inhaled deeply, straightened, and continued down the steps.

She climbed into the cart, and Mark scooted up right next to her until their sides were touching all the way to her feet. He flicked the reins on Flame's backside, and they were off.

After they were a piece down the road, Mark turned to look at her. "It's all right, Mary."

She glanced at him.

"I know it's only natural for you to be looking at Isaac." He swallowed, and his shoulders rose. "Only natural. I'm not upset. Truly. I hope you won't be fretting about it."

Mary's throat tightened. She was stunned that he had brought it up. And he wasn't upset? Such a far cry from not that long ago. Her breath seeped out, and she sagged against him.

"Thank you," she whispered. "It doesn't mean anything, you know."

"I know." His words were clipped, and his attention went back to the road.

It doesn't mean anything.

She could only pray that her words were true.

Chapter Seventeen

The weeks ticked by and December arrived, ushered in with ice and snow.

"I don't want you going out in this, Mary," Mark told her one morning. "It ain't safe. You could slip and fall."

"I been walking in ice and snow since I was little more than a *boppli*," she countered. "I'm fine."

"I can see to everything outside," he said. "You stay in."

Mary grimaced. "I need to gather the eggs."

"Them hens aren't laying much in this cold. Besides, I can check for any eggs."

"All right," she agreed, though she didn't like it. The closed air inside the house sometimes got so dry and stifling that it nearly choked her. She figured she could at least stand out on the porch when it got too bad.

"I'll be back in for the noon meal." He kissed her on the cheek and left.

She stood at the window, watching him slog through the snow to the barn. It wasn't too deep yet. Knowing Indiana weather, it could turn to springlike again by morning and everything would melt. Forty degree jumps or drops in temperature weren't all that unusual. But she supposed they would be socked in for a while.

She turned back to the kitchen and looked at the stack of dirty dishes. She wasn't in the mood to wash them. She scoffed at herself. Since when was being in the mood necessary? She shook her head and walked over to the pile.

Following the work frolic at the Benders', she'd experienced odd pains a few more times. They always passed quickly, so she wasn't unduly concerned, but she reckoned that talking with Old Mae about them wouldn't hurt. She sighed. Since Mark didn't want her out and about on her own, he'd have to drive her over to Old Mae's. Then, what was he going to do? Sit there while she conferred with the healer? Mary didn't like that idea. It wasn't the husband's place to be around during a pregnancy consultation.

She plunged her hands into the soapy water. Maybe, her mother could take her. But Sandra Hochstetler had her hands full with Mary's four brothers still at home. She wondered when her eldest brother John was going to marry and leave the house. Mary had thought that he might do something this wedding season, but there had been no word of anything. He had been baptized, so he was free to be published and married in the church. She used to think he was sweet on Sally Yoder, but nothing had come of it.

Her mind continued to wander as she finished up with the dishes. Afterward, she looked about, knowing she should probably get some bread rising. They were almost finished with her last batch. Instead, she walked to the rocker beside the warming stove and sat down. She wished she liked to knit. That would pass the time nicely. But the last time she'd tried her hand at knitting, she'd spent most of her time pulling stitches out and re-knitting rows upon rows.

It was not pleasant.

She could bake a pie. She had some rich creamy milk and some shredded coconut. A coconut cream pie would be right nice on such a cold day. She got back up and went to the refrigerator. One egg left. That was all. She shut the door and went to the window over the sink. Peering out, she tried to spot Mark. Had he even checked the hen house that day? She felt sure that one or two of the hens had probably laid that morning. Well, in the meantime, she could make a crust.

She had two crusts baked, ready and waiting for the filling within twenty-five minutes. She leaned on the counter, craning against the window, still trying to spot Mark. If she wanted the pies ready for the noon meal, she needed to get on it. Cutting a coconut pie before it was cooled would never work. She sighed and went to the front door, opening it a crack.

It wasn't so cold outside. She stepped out onto the porch. It wasn't really that cold at all. If she was quick, she could be out to the hen house and back with a couple eggs before Mark was done with whatever chores he was doing. In truth, it would save him a chore. She stepped down the first step, testing for ice. Her foot slipped slightly, but she held firmly onto the rail. She scanned the ground. Not bad. She knew how to walk on ice anyway.

A stiff breeze caught her, and she shivered. Maybe, she should put on her cape after all. She went back inside and grabbed her cape from its peg by the door. Better. She stepped gingerly down the steps and started across the yard. She planted each foot carefully, holding her hands out a bit for balance.

She made good progress toward the hen house, which was located to the side of the barn. She arrived and unlatched the door. The hens sent up a chorus of cackles as she stepped inside.

"*Nee*, I don't have food for you," she said with a smile. "I'm just here to collect what's mine."

She laughed at that and stepped aside as one of the hens started pecking her thick black soles through the snow.

"Skedaddle!" She shooed it away. She held onto the wire sides of the pen and made her way to the nesting boxes. The frigid air pinched at her face, and she wondered how on earth she'd thought it wasn't cold outside. Reaching under the straw in the first box, she felt around for eggs. The first two nesting boxes were empty, and she began to think she'd made the trip out there for nothing. But in the third and fourth boxes, she found three eggs.

Cradling them in her hand, she left, being careful to latch the gate securely behind her. The eggs were still warm and felt mighty nice on her cold hands. She walked carefully back toward the house. A sharp cry from a crow overhead grabbed her attention. She looked up, watching it swoop through the air and aim directly for the large maple tree in the middle of the yard.

Mary's foot caught on something, and she lurched, losing her balance. Teetering sideways, she cried out. The eggs! Twisting her body in an attempt to save the eggs, she landed hard on her side, knocking the breath from her lungs. She gasped and sputtered, moaning loudly. Her leg hurt. Her side hurt. Her head hurt.

She tried to sit up, but a sharp pain whipped through her, knocking her back to the frozen ground. The eggs lay broken, smashed and oozing yellow right near her face.

She screwed up her eyes in pain. Something was wrong. This pain was much worse than the other times. She raised her head and desperately looked around.

Chapter Eighteen

"**M**ark!" Mary cried as another pain snatched her voice. She curled on the dirty snow, her hand pressing on her stomach. It hurt. Oh, it hurt.

Where was Mark? Why hadn't he heard her? She sucked in air and blew it out between clenched teeth. In and out. In and out. She closed her eyes. Breathe. That was it. Just breathe.

Mary had no idea how much time had passed, but finally, the pain lessened enough for her to get up. She stumbled back to the house, nearly falling through the front door. She peeled off her cape, let it drop, and hurried up to the bathroom.

Ten minutes later, she was lying on her bed, thanking the Lord. As far as she could tell, she was fine. The baby was fine. There was no bleeding. Nothing to indicate anything was wrong. She pulled up a quilt and lay still, letting her heart slow and her breathing return to normal.

The front door opened, and she could hear Mark's heavy footsteps.

"Mary?" he called. "Where are you?"

"Up here," she answered, forcing her voice to sound normal.

He climbed the stairs and came into their bedroom. "You're in bed? Are you tired?"

She nodded.

"The strangest thing…" he said, coming to sit on the edge of the bed. "I found eggs all broken and smashed on the ground. If some critter got into the hen house, them eggs would have been devoured. I couldn't find any evidence of—"

Mary covered her mouth with her hand. Shame flooded her, and her misery was like a steel weight.

"Mary, what is it?"

"Me…" she cried. "It was me."

She felt him go stiff.

"You broke them eggs?"

She nodded, feeling wretched.

"But that would mean you went outside." He stood and faced her. "I asked you not to go out. What happened? Why are you in bed?"

Tears dripped down her face. She'd never been so ashamed. She'd disobeyed her husband and put the baby and herself in jeopardy. And all for a few eggs? She blinked back her tears and swallowed.

"Mary? What did you do?" His voice sharpened.

"I wanted t-to make a coconut pie," she said, sniffling. "I needed eggs, and I couldn't see you—"

"I told you I'd check for the eggs."

"I know, but…" She wiped her face. "I'm sorry."

"What happened?"

"I fell."

He sucked in his breath and sank down beside her.

He took her hand. "Are you all right? Did you hurt your-self?"

"I'm fine." She clamped her lips shut. She didn't dare tell him about the shooting pain. What had she been thinking? Had her brain gone to mush with this pregnancy?

He studied her face. "You're sure you're all right."

"I'm sorry," she uttered. "Truly. I'm sorry."

He squeezed her hand. "I guess no harm's done. But you didn't get your eggs, did you?"

She gave him a small smile. "*Nee*. I didn't get my eggs."

"You want me to go fetch some from the neighbors for you?"

She shook her head. She didn't have an ounce of energy left to make any old pie.

He stood and looked down at her tenderly. "I'll fix the noon meal. Do you want me to get your *mamm*? Or Old Mae?"

Mary thought on that. She'd been wanting to see Old Mae anyway. Maybe now was as good a time as any. "Can you get Old Mae for me?"

His expression darkened. "But you're okay?"

"*Jah*. I was going to go see her today or tomorrow anyway."

"You were? You never mentioned it."

"I was going to have *Mamm* take me."

"I'll go get Old Mae. Of course, I'll get her." He walked to the doorway and paused. "You'll be all right while I'm gone."

She smiled. "*Jah*. I'm fine. Take your time."

But after he left, Mary felt anxious. Nervous, even. She was mighty glad she'd sent him for Old Mae. Something felt off. Gingerly, she reached down and felt along her ankles and legs, wondering if she'd bruised them in her fall. Nothing hurt, but she still felt off. She checked her arms and felt a soreness on one of her elbows. That was going to hurt worse tomorrow, she knew.

She closed her eyes and tried to relax. She turned on her side and punched at her pillow, trying to get more comfortable. She kicked off the quilt and then pulled it back up again. A metallic taste filled her mouth, but she had no urge to vomit. A dull ache filled her stomach. Was she hungry? She could go down and grab something to eat. She shifted to get up but changed her mind. She didn't want to move. Her body felt like dead weight.

She glanced at the wind-up clock on her bedside stand.

Hurry up, Mark. Bring Old Mae quickly.

She concentrated on her breath. She'd heard Deborah say that breathing in a slow rhythm helped calm a person. But it didn't work. She changed position again, wishing the pain in her stomach would lessen. Instead, it was increasing.

No. It wasn't hunger.

She sighed nervously. *Hurry up, Mark.*

Chapter Nineteen

Mary jerked awake with a start. Frantically, her eyes jolted around the room. What had awakened her? What was going on? She remained still and tried to clear her head. Something was wrong. She felt warm. Very warm. But not all over. Just between her legs. With a desperate cry, she threw off the quilt and looked down. She was lying in a puddle of blood.

"*Nee!*" she shrieked. Her dress was drenched and plastered to her legs. "*Nee!*"

She struggled to a sitting position, still gaping down at herself. Blood. Blood was everywhere. It could only mean one thing. Her voice wrenched from her throat in a crushing sob.

"My boppli!"

Agonizing pain grabbed her, and she bent double. She screamed when the pain came again and again. When it finally stopped, she inched herself to the edge of the bed. She slung her legs over the side. Blood trickled down her thighs and over her knees. No. No. No. She stumbled up and started down the hallway to the bathroom, leaning crazily into the wall. She gasped and sputtered as she burst into the bathroom.

She heard commotion downstairs. *Mark*. He was back. She heard Old Mae's sharp voice saying something. She didn't know what. Her brain was fuzzy. Her legs buckled, and she fell onto the floor.

"Mark!" she called, but her voice was weak.

She heard them come up the stairs.

"She's resting," Mark was saying. "I'll just let you go on—" His voice went silent. Then, "Mary! Mary!"

He erupted through the bathroom door, took one horrified look at her on the floor and dropped beside her. "Mae!" he screamed. "In here! Mae!"

Mary looked up desperately at him. "It'll be okay. Won't it?" she begged him. "Won't it?" She grabbed his sleeve.

Old Mae peered through the door. She took one look, and her expression tightened. "Mark. Leave us. I'll take over now."

Mark looked helplessly at the old woman. "But—"

"You heard me," Old Mae commanded. "Leave us."

Mark got up and backed out of the bathroom, his eyes wide and his features twisted. Old Mae quickly shut the door. She reached down and pulled Mary into a sitting position.

"There, there," she crooned. "Let's get you cleaned up."

"The *boppli*…" Mary wailed. "The *boppli*… She'll be all right, won't she?" Even as she spoke, Mary knew she was grasping at air. How could her baby possibly be all right? The truth bore into her. *Nothing, nothing, nothing* would ever be all right again.

"I'm here," Old Mae told her as she gently unfastened Mary's dress. "*Gott* is here."

"My...*boppli*," Mary whispered. She bent over and wailed. Old Mae sank to the floor and held her.

"There, there," Old Mae hummed in her ear. "There, there."

Mary burrowed into Old Mae's bony shoulder. Despair filled her until she thought she would choke on it. She could barely breathe. Sobs gushed up her throat.

She had done this. She had *killed her own baby.*

"I-I..." She wanted to tell Old Mae. She wanted to see the censure on her face. She wanted to be punished. She had done this. "I went for eggs outside. I-I fell..."

"Shh now," Old Mae said. She pulled on Mary's sleeves, peeling off her dress. It was difficult as Mary couldn't seem to move to be of any help.

Old Mae grunted softly, maneuvering Mary's body as best she could. When the dress was off, Mary gaped down at her undergarments, soaked in blood. Another wave of grief swept over her, and her cries increased.

"Now, now, go ahead and cry it out. That's a *gut* girl. Get it out." Mae stood and took a washcloth from the towel rack. She ran it under the tap and brought it to wipe Mary's face. The rag was cool and Mary hiccupped as she sobbed.

"I'm going to draw a bath," Mae said. "We'll get you cleaned up. Then I'm going to tuck you into bed and bring you a nice hot cup of tea."

Old Mae's watery gray eyes looked into hers. "You're going to be all right," she stated. "I promise. You're going to be all right."

"My *boppli*..." Mary said again, her voice catching.

How could she have been so stupid? How could she have disobeyed her husband? She had *killed her baby.*

Old Mae busied herself over the tub, getting it ready. Mary sat, slumped against the wall, trying to breathe. Trying to understand. Trying to grasp the horror of what she'd done.

"All right, Mary." Old Mae turned to her. She bent down and grabbed Mary under her arms, urging her to a standing position. "Help me a bit. I'm strong, but I'm old. Come on, now. Up you go. There. There you are."

Mary stood, shivering violently. Old Mae pulled off her undergarments until Mary stood before her naked. Mary couldn't remember ever standing before someone like that. No one saw her naked. Even Mark rarely saw her naked.

Old Mae put her arm around Mary's back and led her to the tub. "Step in. Come on. There you go. Now, sit down. I'm going to wash you."

Mary gave Mae a pleading look. "Is the *boppli* really gone? Can't we go to the *Englisch* hospital? Can't we? Maybe the *boppli* is fine. We don't know for sure."

Old Mae sighed and the look of compassion on her face nearly did Mary in. "The *boppli* is with *Gott* now, child. She's warm and safe in the Father's arms."

"But... I wanted her warm and safe in *my* arms." Mary leaned against the side of the tub and started crying again.

Old Mae kneeled by the tub and plunged the washrag into the warm water. Gently, she washed Mary's body. Gently, she rinsed her by squeezing the water out of the rag over her skin.

There was a knock on the door.

"Mae?" Mark said. "Is Mary all right in there? Is everything okay?"

Mae turned toward the door. "We're all right, Mark. I'm washing Mary up. We'll be out shortly."

Mary stared ahead. Mark would hate her. He would hate her until the end of time.

"There will be other *bopplis*," Old Mae said softly. "I know that ain't no comfort right now, but it's the way of things. This first one will always have a piece of your heart. But there will be others. Many, many others."

Mary looked at her dully and blinked. "There won't be others," she said. "*Gott* will punish me."

"For what, child? For going outside to fetch eggs? For falling? *Gott* won't be punishing you for that."

Mary pulled back her lips. "I disobeyed my husband."

Old Mae didn't even flinch. "*Gott* won't be punishing you," she said again, more firmly.

"Didn't you hear what I said?" Mary asked, her voice rising. Didn't the woman realize what she'd done? Was she daft?

"Mary Schrock. Did *you* hear *me*? I'm telling you that you didn't harm this *boppli*. *Gott* called her home. These things happen."

Mary shook her head. *"Nee. Nee."*

"Jah, they do. I'm an old woman, Mary. I've seen this happen more times than I care to count. That precious little *boppli* is in *Gott's* arms. Don't you doubt *Gott's* will."

"But…" Mary stared right into Old Mae's face. The woman didn't understand. She simply didn't get it. But Mary knew. She knew what she'd done. She knew that if she hadn't gone outside, her baby would still be alive.

"You haven't been to see me lately," Old Mae said, rinsing Mary's back.

"I planned to go today."

"You been having any strange pains? Anything out of the ordinary?"

Mary frowned.

Old Mae nodded. "As I thought. It wasn't your fall that did it, girl. These things happen."

Mary continued to stare at her. Her breath came in shallows bursts. Could it be true? Could it be that her fall hadn't done it? No. She knew better. Old Mae could say whatever she wanted, but it wouldn't change the truth of it.

There was another knock at the door.

"Mae?" Mark's voice sounded choked and warbled through the door. It didn't sound like him at all.

Old Mae pulled the plug. "You'll bleed for a while, and I don't want you worrying about that. I'm going to let Mark dry you and get you to bed. I'll go down and fix the tea."

"Nee!" Mary cried, panicked. She clutched Old Mae's arm. *"You* dry me. *Please."*

She didn't want to see Mark. She didn't want to see the devastation and accusation on his face. She couldn't bear it.

Old Mae hesitated. She studied Mary's face. "I'm going down to fix the tea." She turned and opened the door. Mark must have been leaning on it because he nearly toppled over her.

"Get her dry and into bed," Mae said calmly. "She'll bleed for a while." She gathered up Mary's soiled clothing and left the room.

Mary drew her knees up to her chin and put her arms

around her shaking body. She looked down at the tub, fighting to hold in her anguish.

"Mary?" Mark whispered.

She didn't respond.

"Mary? I brought you some clean clothes." Mark knelt on the floor by her side. He tried to peel her arms from about her legs, but she resisted. Her limbs had become cement, and she was glad. She didn't want him to see her—all of her. She didn't want him to see her naked without the baby inside of her.

"Mary?" He was pleading with her now. "I need to get you up and dressed. You're shivering. Let me help you."

The tenderness in his voice raked through her like jagged nails. She flinched and leaned away from him.

"Mary!" More firmly now. "I'm getting you out of this tub. You can help me or not. I have to get you dressed and warm. You're cold, Mary."

I'm frozen, she thought dully. *I'm made of ice.*

Mark reached into the tub, grabbing her around the shoulders. With brute stubbornness, he raised her to a standing position. She stood, surprised that her legs worked. She kept her arms around herself, trying to cover herself, wondering if she was going to leave a trail of blood.

"Mary, step up and out now. I can lift you if you need me to. But you'd probably be more comfortable if you stepped out on your own."

Mary stared down at her trembling legs. She looked at her feet, standing in the small bloodied puddle of water in the bottom of the tub. She blinked and experimented with lifting one foot. It came up, and she swung it stiffly over the side of the tub.

"There you go," Mark said. She was still in his arms,

and he helped her onto the braided rug. "I'll dry you off, and then I'll get you dressed."

Mary stared at the wall while Mark managed to dress her. When he was finished, he opened the door and with his arm around her, led her back to the bedroom. When they entered, her eyes flew to the bed. It was still covered with blood. Her favorite quilt—the wedding pattern quilt her mother had made for her—was completely ruined. She gasped and slumped against Mark.

He sucked in his breath and quickly led her out of the room and into a spare bedroom. Mary's throat swelled into a hard lump. This was to be the nursery. The baby's cradle, the one Mark had so painstakingly crafted, sat empty in the corner. There was a narrow bed against the opposite wall.

"I'm sorry to bring you in here, Mary," Mark said, his voice stiff and thick. "It's just for a bit. I'll clean up our room."

He tucked her into the bed and looked down at her for a minute before leaving. Mary stared at the ceiling. She was heavy. *So heavy.* It made no sense. Her baby was gone. How could she be heavy? She tried to raise her arm beneath the covers. It wouldn't move. She blinked up at the ceiling. Odd. Maybe she was dead, too.

Was this how it felt to be dead? Cold. Heavy. Immobile.

It wasn't terribly unpleasant. And if she was dead, she would be done with all of this, wouldn't she? That was a nice thought. To be done.

She heard Mark in the room across the hall. The room that was *their* bedroom. She heard him changing the bedding. Would he burn the quilt?

What did it matter?

How curious it was to lie there, staring but not seeing, hearing but not listening… Such an odd sensation. She licked her lips, trying to taste.

Nothing.

She closed her eyes and went to sleep.

Chapter Twenty

It was dark when Mary opened her eyes. It took a moment before reality rushed in and grabbed her by the throat. She cried out and turned on her side, curling into a ball.

"Mary?" Mark's voice came through the darkness. She heard him fumble about and then the lantern was lit. "You're awake."

He bent close and rubbed his hand over her hair. Was her *kapp* still on? A lock of hair fell over her forehead, so she knew it wasn't. Who had taken her *kapp* off and let down her hair?

"Old Mae has gone home. I had to get the Allens to take her. I didn't want to leave you. She gave me some herbal tea for you. Do you want a cup? I can have it ready in a flash."

Talking. So much talking. Mary shook her head and tried to swallow. Her throat hurt. It was too dry.

"Mary?"

"*Nee*," she choked out. "No tea."

"It might taste *gut*. Are you hungry? I can get something for you."

Still talking. She closed her eyes.

"*Jah*. That's it. You sleep some more. You'll feel better in the morning."

Feel better? Was he insane? She was never going to feel better. And what was wrong with him? Why was he being nice to her? Didn't he know what she'd done? Didn't he know that she'd killed their baby?

She turned over.

"Mary? You sure I can't get anything for you?" And then she heard it. A hitch beneath his words. Something a bit off.

She opened her eyes and stared back at him. In the flickering light, he blanched slightly at her intense gaze.

"I will leave," she said. "Don't worry."

He backed up a step. "What do you mean? You'll leave to where?"

"To away from here," she said dully. He didn't want her. She could hear it now. He wasn't insane at all; he knew perfectly well what she'd done. She let out her breath. It was almost a relief to hear that tone in his voice. The accusation.

And it would be a relief to leave.

"You're not making sense," he said, moving forward to tuck the quilt about her. "We'll talk more in the morning." He looked around the room. "I'll sit in the rocker tonight, so if you need me, I'll be near."

"*Nee.*"

His brow furrowed. "*Nee?*"

"Go to bed. What did you do with the quilt?"

"I-I...didn't know what to do. It's downstairs."

"Go to bed. We'll talk in the morning."

He gave her a doubtful look. "I don't mind staying in here with you."

"*Nee*."

He blew out his breath. "Fine. I'll be across the hall then."

Mary turned toward the wall and waited stiffly for him to leave. It was a minute or two before his footsteps finally sounded, trudging to the door and out of the room. She exhaled. She would leave the next day. She could go to the phone shanty and call the Mennonite driver they often used. The same one Mark had used to go to the auction.

And where was she going?

She had no idea. No earthly idea.

But somewhere. Anywhere.

She closed her eyes and knotted her fists beneath her chin. Tomorrow. Yes.

Tomorrow, she would leave.

Mary opened her eyes to the gentle light falling into the room through the window. She blinked and focused.

"You're awake," her mother said, rising from the rocking chair next to the cradle.

"*Mamm*?"

Sandra Hochstetler smiled tenderly at her. "*Jah*, it's me. Mark came to fetch me last night."

"You've been here all night."

She stifled a yawn and stretched. "I have."

"There was no need," Mary flinched at the sound of her own harsh tone. "I mean. I'm fine."

"You're not fine." Sandra plumped the pillows beneath Mary's head. "You need some time is all. I'm here to help out."

"You have enough to do already."

Sandra chuckled. "That I do. But I'm your *mamm*, and I'm not going anywhere for a couple days."

Mary shoved the quilts off and sat up, scooting back against the headboard. "I'm leaving today."

Sandra's brow shot up. "Leaving? Where are you going?"

"I don't know. I thought maybe *Aenti* could use some help?"

"My sister? In Linnow Creek? Why in the world do you want to go see her?"

Mary inhaled sharply. "I just do."

"That's nonsense. You'll stay here and recover. You'll be right as rain in a couple days. You just wait and see."

Mary eyed her mother. Right as rain in a couple days? And why hadn't her mother mentioned the dead baby? She was treating her as if she had the stomach flu or something.

"*Mamm.* I'm going. You know *Aenti* will welcome me."

Sandra's breath hissed out in a sigh. "Well, of course, she'll welcome you. That's not the point. You can't leave. You need to rest, and what about Mark? You going to just up and leave him?"

"Mark is fine. And it's not like I'm *leaving* leaving him. Just for a spell. Not forever."

Although, right then, the thought of never seeing Mark again, never looking into his eyes again, held a certain appeal. But she could hardly even breathe such words to her mother.

"I don't like it. Your *dat* won't like it."

Mary relaxed her face into what she hoped was a pleasant expression. She took a slow, even breath. "*Mamm*, I need to get away for a few days. That's all.

Being away will help me heal. I promise I'll be back right soon."

Sandra studied her. She was quiet for a long moment. "It's not done," she finally said.

"What do you mean?"

"A wife traipsing off like that."

"I'm not traipsing off. I'm visiting my *aenti* who could use my help."

Her mother pursed her lips. "I suppose if we put it like that…"

Mary saw her advantage and pushed. "Can you call Naomi for me? Tell her I'll be there as soon as I can."

"You want *me* to call her?"

"Please."

"I'm not telling Mark for you. He needs to hear this wild plan from your lips."

Mary put her hand on her mother's arm. "It's not a wild plan. And thank you, *Mamm*. Thank you for helping me."

Sandra shook her head, her forehead creased with doubt. "I don't know…"

Mary shifted in bed, testing her body a bit. Checking to see how she felt. She was stiff, but she knew that was from the fall, not from…well, not from…losing the baby. She winced against the rush of pain roaring through her heart. She adjusted her expression and wriggled to the side of the bed.

"Do you want help dressing?" Sandra asked her.

"*Nee*. I'm fine." Mary put her feet onto the rag rug beside the bed and stood. So far, so good.

"I'll get breakfast."

"Thank you."

Her mother left. Mary moved across the hall to her

bedroom. She took her time removing her nightgown and putting on her dress. She moved slowly, carefully, almost as if she were afraid to touch herself. She glanced under the bed and saw the suitcase that was so rarely used. She knelt down and pulled it out. She would need to get packed if she was leaving today.

She had just opened the suitcase on the bed when she heard someone taking the steps two at a time. *Mark.* He rarely hurried up the stairs like that, but he was rushing now. He burst into their room.

"You're really going, then?" he asked, staring at her.

"I-I… I told you last night that I was going."

He didn't move. "That was last night. I thought that this morning…"

"You thought wrong. I'm going to Linnow Creek to help *Aenti* Naomi."

"She doesn't need your help."

Mary pinched her lips together. He was likely right. Her aunt didn't need any help. But Mary didn't know what else to say. Inside, she was crying out for escape. Wailing to leave. How could she tell him that?

He took two steps closer. "Mary. Please, don't go."

Tears pricked her eyes. She looked into his face, searching for what he might be thinking, what he was feeling. She saw his pain, but she knew it wasn't for her. Of course, it wasn't for her. He was asking her to stay, but she couldn't. She simply couldn't.

He reached out and touched her arm. His fingers lingered, burning through the fabric of her sleeves. He stepped closer.

"Don't go."

She drew in a shaky breath. "I have to. I have to go."

His expression hardened, and he dropped his hand. "What am I going to say? How can I explain this?"

Her heart went cold. So that was it? That was why he wanted her to stay? So he wouldn't have to explain her absence?

"I'm going to help my *aenti*. There is nothing more to explain."

"You're leaving me?"

She blew out her breath. "I'll be back."

They stared at each other. Mary looked into his hooded eyes and knew he was regretting their marriage. What had she given him? A smoothly-running home? Yes. That. But the deep love he hoped for...? The child he wanted...?

"I'm sorry," she choked out.

His eyes narrowed. "So am I." He turned on his heel and left the room.

Chapter Twenty-One

❧

Mary sat in the back of the van, completely numb. Getting out of the house with her mother hovering and Mark hanging back, was excruciating. Now, she perched on the vinyl seat, her seatbelt fastened around her newly flattened stomach. She stared blindly out the window as the scenery passed in a blur.

Naomi didn't know she was coming. Her mother had called to the closest phone shanty in Linnow Creek, but no one had answered.

No matter. Her aunt would welcome her.

Old Mae would probably stop by the house today and be surprised to find her gone. Mary hadn't even said good-bye to Deborah. She gave a heavy sigh. Deborah would already know by now. Everyone in the district probably already knew; that was how fast the gossip train worked in the area.

She knew that the driver, Amos, kept glancing back at her using the mirror in the middle of the front window. She didn't wonder. Her farewell had been so awkward that he had to know something was wrong.

It didn't matter.

She leaned back against the seat and tried to relax. In a couple hours, she'd be there. In a different world. Away from everything. And it would be better.

It had to be.

"Mary Hochstetler, what a surprise," Naomi exclaimed when Mary climbed out of the van.

"It's Mary Schrock now, remember?" Mary said, feeling stiff and achy.

Naomi leaned around her, peering into the van. "Is Sandra with you?"

"*Nee. Mamm's* at home."

One of Naomi's brows arched at this piece of news, but she didn't question it. "Come right on in. Won't Ezra be pleased to see you."

Mary hoped so. She allowed Naomi to snatch up her bag and lead her inside. Naomi's home was not so different from theirs. Many Amish homes looked quite similar inside. And they all had large dining areas, which was where Naomi led her.

"You must be hungry after your trip."

Mary hadn't eaten much of anything since before her fall. Her stomach ached, and she had no appetite.

"*Nee*. I'm fine, *Aenti*."

"Nonsense," Naomi said. "Sit down and I'll get you some nice hot tea and a fresh cinnamon roll."

Mary sat and wondered how she'd possibly choke down a cinnamon roll. However, she did have to admit that the sweet smell of sugar and spice wafting from the kitchen was pleasant.

Naomi laughed. "If my *kinner* were still around, these rolls would already be gone. As it is, Ezra doesn't even know they're ready."

"How are my cousins?" Mary asked.

"Right *gut*. Every last one of them." Naomi had gone into the kitchen now and was fussing with the faucet.

Mary heard the water pouring into the tea kettle. And then came a light clatter of dishes. Naomi reappeared. "Thought I'd have one with you," she said with a wink. "Eating a fresh cinnamon roll doesn't require much of an excuse, now, does it?"

Mary nodded. Her aunt didn't look a day older than when she'd seen her six months or so ago. She was the eldest in her mother's family, so she was considerably older than Sandra. Her hair was mostly white, pulled back tightly under her *kapp*. Her striking blue eyes darted about, not missing a thing. But it was her voice that Mary liked best. It was rich and warm, and when she spoke, it was almost as if she were singing.

Naomi set the rolls down and chatted easily about her eight children. The kettle began to whistle, and she jumped up from the table and bustled back into the kitchen. In three minutes, she was back with two steaming cups. She set one before Mary.

"Here you are, child."

Mary smiled and put her hands around the cup, soaking in its warmth.

"Now," Naomi said and situated herself into her chair, "suppose you tell me what this is all about."

Mary tensed and didn't look at her.

"You are welcome to stay here as long as you like. Your cousins will be delighted to see you. But you didn't just come to pass the time of day. What has happened?"

Mary fought the tears burning at the backs of her eyes. She swallowed and her nostrils flared.

"Mary? You can tell your old *aenti*. What is it?"

"I-I…" Mary tried to get the words out, but they wouldn't come. She looked over at Naomi, helpless.

Naomi patted her arm. "Take a sip or two of that hot tea. It'll loosen your tongue. And there ain't no hurry. We've got all day, if you like."

The ache in Mary's stomach increased, crawling up her throat until she thought she would vomit. She blinked rapidly and tried to swallow it back down.

"*Ach*, Mary, I see you're hurting." Naomi got up and stood beside her, resting her hand on Mary's shoulder. "Would you like to go into the front room? Sit in a rocker?"

Mary shook her head. The tears spilled over her eyes and down her cheeks.

"I-I lost my *boppli*…" she eked out.

Naomi let out a soft gasp and tightened her grip on Mary's shoulder. "There, there," she crooned, not leaving her side.

"It was my fault," Mary continued, her voice pinched and forced.

She felt Naomi stiffen. And then the woman backed away a step. She leaned down, putting her face close to Mary's. "What do you mean your fault?"

Mary shook her head. The tears continued to fall. Naomi reached back and grabbed her chair, pulling it close to Mary. She sat again, and peeled Mary's clenched hands from the teacup and held onto them.

"Suppose you tell me what happened?" Naomi said softly.

Mary looked at her through her tears and nodded. With a shuddering voice, she told her aunt everything. Naomi didn't interrupt her once. She only clicked her tongue a few times against her teeth in a sound of sympathy. When Mary finished, Naomi leaned against the back of her chair.

"That is a sad story, for sure and for certain." Her eyes were full of compassion. "I'm right sorry you had to go through that. But it weren't your fault, child."

"But it was! I disobeyed. I went outside and fell."

"That little *boppli* is right where she should be. In *Gott's* arms."

"But—"

Naomi held up her hand, silencing her. "Mary, I want to tell you something." She paused, and her expression tightened. "Your *mamm* doesn't even know what I'm about to tell you."

Mary wiped her face with a napkin. What was Naomi going to tell her? Whatever it was, it was obviously painful.

"I lost two *bopplis* early in my marriage."

Mary's eyes widened.

"No one knew. Just me and Ezra." She inhaled deeply. "It about killed me. *Jah*, it about did me in. Two babes. Lost. Right in a row, too." She shook her head. "Was the hardest thing I've ever lived through."

Empathy flooded Mary. She gripped her aunt's hand.

"It were a long time ago. It still hurts. But it's a different kind of hurt now. Almost a sweet sorrow. Oh, I know you can't know what I mean. It's too soon yet. But someday, you will." She scooted her cup of tea away from her. "I know my precious little ones are with *Gott*. Someday, I hope to see them."

She looked at Mary then, her eyes brimming with tears. "You'll get through this. I promise you that. *Gott* is faithful. He'll heal you and help you. Don't ever hesitate to lean on him."

Mary nodded.

Twice…? Naomi had gone through this twice. But at least, she hadn't been at fault. Unlike her. And it sounded like Ezra was right there with her, helping her and loving her. She dropped her eyes, sure that she would never have that. Perhaps she hadn't given Mark a fair chance. In reality, she hadn't. But she'd seen that look in his eyes. She'd seen the truth.

He did blame her. And she knew that hatred would follow right behind the blame.

"What does your husband say about this?" Naomi asked. "Was he in favor of you leaving?"

Mary gulped, not wanting to tell the truth. But she could hardly lie, could she?

"He wanted me to stay," she murmured.

"So, why did you leave?"

Mary let go of Naomi's hand and stood up so quickly, she nearly knocked the bench over behind her. "I had to. I had to leave. He blames me, too."

Naomi regarded her for a long minute. "So, you didn't honor his wishes."

Hot anger surged through Mary. "I shouldn't have come. This was wrong."

Naomi stood up. "*Nee*, child. You should have come. You're a confused mess of emotions right now and understandably so. Give yourself some time. It will be easier, soon."

Mary's anger faded slightly. She realized that she was shaking.

"Now, this is what you're going to do. You're going to sit back down and eat something. Then I'm going to take you upstairs and tuck you into your cousin Greta's old bed. You're going to take a nice long rest until suppertime. Then, I'll come and fetch you, and you and me and Ezra will have a quiet meal together."

Mary nodded. It was good not to have to decide anything. She sat back down and picked up a cinnamon roll.

Chapter Twenty-Two

Mary slept well. When Naomi came to fetch her for supper, she was surprised to find that she had slept the entire afternoon away.

"Feeling any better?" Naomi asked on their way down the stairs.

Mary wasn't sure. But upon smelling the food, she did notice that she was hungry. She supposed that was progress.

"Ezra's mighty glad you're here," Naomi said.

They went to the table and Ezra greeted Mary with a big smile. "Mary Hochstetler. How *gut* to see you again."

"Mary Schrock," she corrected him, just as she'd corrected her aunt.

"*Jah, jah*. Of course." His expression turned serious. "Right sorry I was to hear of your loss."

"Thank you," she responded softly.

"You came to the right place," he said. "Naomi's been wanting some female company these days. What with the *kinner* gone and the days growing mighty cold, it gets a bit lonesome around here."

Naomi gave him a playful swat on the arm. "Ezra! You don't need to be telling tales, now."

"I ain't telling no tales. You told me the other day how much you missed having someone else around this house." He leaned toward Mary and winked. "She's right sick of me, I suppose."

"Ezra!" Naomi exclaimed.

Mary smiled.

"Let's bow for the blessing," Ezra instructed. "Shall we?"

Mary bowed her head and attempted to pray, but her mind wouldn't settle. She wondered if she would sleep that night, considering how long she'd slept during the day. She wondered whether Naomi had any sewing projects she could help with. She wondered what would have happened if she'd followed Isaac to the *Englisch* world.

She winced. Where had that thought come from? Yet if she had followed Isaac, and if she had been pregnant in the fancy world, she would have gone to a hospital. She would have been seen by an *Englisch* doctor from the very start. And maybe, just maybe, she would still have her baby.

She knew that *Englisch* doctors could perform miracles.

Ezra cleared his throat. The blessing was over. "Pass me them beans," he said to his wife.

Later that evening, Mary sat on the edge of her bed in the candlelight. She held her tablet and pencil. She needed to write to Deborah. Her friend would wonder if the rumors were true, and she'd probably be vexed that Mary hadn't come to tell her personally what had happened. Mary figured that a letter was the next best thing.

She'd been trying to write it for nearly half an hour. Everything she put down, sounded whiny and awful.

She also tried to write to Mark, yet absolutely nothing came forth. She had a sudden urge to write to Isaac, but she didn't dare put pencil to paper for that. Writing an old beau would be terribly wrong. And terribly unfair to Mark.

She sighed heavily, determined to write her dear friend.

Dear Deborah,
By now, you probably know that I have left Hollybrook for a bit. You probably also know why.

Mary's throat constricted, and she tried to swallow. She couldn't keep on breaking down every time she thought of her lost child. Hadn't she run out of tears yet? She blew out her breath and continued writing.

I am with my aenti and onkel here. I'll be staying for a while and helping my aenti. I'm sorry I wasn't able to visit with you before I left. It was a right quick decision.
When I come back, I'll visit you as soon as I can.
With love, your friend,
Mary

Mary reread her letter. It basically said nothing, and she knew it. But it was the best she could do for now. She folded it up and slipped it into an envelope. She pressed a stamp onto the corner and addressed the envelope.

She got up and wandered to the window. The sky

looked heavy with snow. The naked branches below swayed gently, so a wind must be blowing. She leaned her head against the wooden frame. A bird was perched at the top of the tree. It looked to be a robin, but she couldn't be sure.

She wondered how Mark was doing. Was he missing her? Or was he secretly glad she was gone? She glanced back at her bed and at her tablet lying open. She needed to write to him. They hadn't parted well.

Reluctantly, she went back and picked up her pad again, sitting down.

Dear Mark,
I hope you are doing well. I'm sorry I left so abruptly. I'm sorry for everything. Naomi and Ezra have welcomed me in, and I'm going to be helping Naomi.
I will come back. I don't know when.
Be well.
Mary

Mary stared down at the letter. It was horrible. But still, she folded it up and put it in an envelope. She placed a stamp in the corner and wrote the address. Then she took up both letters and was about to head downstairs when she remembered that Naomi would probably be upset that she wasn't sleeping.

It wouldn't make much difference if she waited. The postman wasn't going to stop by in the middle of the night. She'd put the letters in the mailbox the next day.

Mary mailed the letters the next morning. And then Naomi got her busy making a new dress. Mary was pleased, as she enjoyed sewing. She was good at it, too; although, she'd never say so aloud. Naomi set her up in the sewing room and popped her head in every now and again.

"How's it going?" Naomi asked in the early afternoon.

"Right well," Mary said. "The pieces are cut, and I've got the bodice about finished."

"Sleeves next?"

Mary nodded. "Sleeves next."

Naomi entered the room and stood next to Mary. "And how are you doing?"

Mary set the fabric down in her lap. "All right." She hadn't cried once that morning, so that was something.

"I'm glad." Naomi fingered the bodice. "This looks nice."

Mary smiled. "Thank you."

"Supper tonight will be a bit late. Ezra had to go into town to fetch some goat feed."

"That's fine."

"All right. I'll leave you to it, then." Naomi squeezed Mary's shoulder and left.

Mary watched her go. Her aunt moved slowly, but with no sign of frailty. She walked with a certain grace, a rhythm that exuded peace. Mary wondered if she would ever be like that. Calm. Serene. Content. She gazed down at her sewing and felt a sudden urge to take a break. She got up and wandered about the room. There wasn't much in there. Nothing really in the way of decoration. Although, there were a few different sizes of doilies spread about. Mary knew her aunt crocheted, and her work was lovely.

She glanced out the window and saw that the snow never arrived. The clouds still hung low and heavy.

Maybe it was about to rain. Mary stretched and decided that some fresh air would do her good.

She left the room and found Naomi in the kitchen.

"I think I'll go for a short walk," she told her.

Naomi turned from the sink. "It's getting cold out there."

"I don't mind. I'll bundle up well."

"Do you want me to come with you?"

Mary shook her head. "*Nee, Aenti*. I'll be fine. Just a short walk."

"All right. If you turn to your right out at the road and walk a short piece, you'll find a small creek. It's real pretty."

"That sounds nice. I'll go there."

"But come right back. I don't want you getting too chilled."

Chapter Twenty-Three

Mary smiled at Naomi and went to put on her heavy cape and scarf. Sometimes she got tired of her thick black shoes, but she had to admit that they did a good job keeping her feet warm during the winter months. The only time she wore boots was when the snow was thick and deep. She pushed open the side door and stepped outside.

The cold air slapped at her face, and she sucked in a long breath. She hadn't realized just how cold it was. She shrank down inside her cape and set out across the yard. Once she got moving, the cold didn't feel so bad. She walked out onto the road and turned right. She hadn't taken two steps when she heard her name.

"Maria?"

She froze, not believing her ears. It couldn't be. It simply *couldn't*. She was afraid to turn around.

"Maria? It's me."

She turned slowly to face Isaac. He gave her such a look of compassion and tenderness, that she barely stopped herself from bursting into tears. He'd come? He'd come all the way to Linnow Creek to see her? And how had he gotten there? She glanced around but saw no van. Nor a driver. Her heart pounded against her ribs at the impossibility of it all. She felt weak.

He rushed to her side, putting his arm around her waist. "Maria. I'm sorry. Forgive me, but I had to come. I had to see you."

She gaped at him with her heart in her throat. "Wh-what are you doing here?"

He led her into a small grove of pine trees. "I heard what happened. Maria, I'm so sorry."

"B-but, I don't understand… What are you *doing* here?" She knew she was gawking at him. Was she hallucinating? Had she lost her mind? But his arm, planted firmly around her waist, felt real enough.

"When I found out you'd left Hollybrook, I had to see you for myself. I found out from one of your brothers where you'd gone. I had to know you were all right." Isaac gazed down at her. "Are you? Are you all right, Maria?"

"You shouldn't be with me. How did you get here? Did you use a van?" She stared at him. "Ike? Are you really here?"

He laughed, and the sound was low and resonant. "I'm really here. Don't be angry with me. I had to see you."

"But you have no right…" She couldn't stop the words, but once they were said, she wished she could grab them back.

His face went dark. "I know that. Don't you think I know that, Maria?" He shook his head. "I made the stupidest mistake of my life, and now, I'm paying for it. You don't have to tell me again."

She blinked, knowing she should bat away his arm,

but it felt so familiar, so comforting that she merely stood, staring into his face, so close to hers. Too close.

She began to shiver, not sure if it was because of the cold air or because she was standing next to the man she thought she'd spend the rest of her life with. She only knew that she couldn't stop trembling, nor could she stop the feeling of things slipping completely out of her control.

"You lost your *boppli*." Isaac touched her cheek with breath-taking gentleness. "I'm sorry."

She blanched at his touch on her face and worked to wriggle out from his arm. "You need to go, Ike. Please."

He held up his hands. "I will. I promise. As soon as I know you're okay."

"Where will the van come pick you up? Did the driver know you were here to see me?"

"*Nee*." Isaac looked down for a long minute before raising his eyes to hers again. "You needn't worry about a driver. I drove myself."

"What?"

"I drove myself. I have a license. I've had one for years. You know that."

"But—"

"I borrowed a car from an *Englisch* friend in Hollybrook." He frowned slightly. "Don't look so horrified, Maria. It was the fastest way I knew to get to you."

Mary wrapped her arms around herself and pressed hard against her stomach, trying to stop the shaking. "You can't be here. You can't."

"I know that." Isaac took hold of both her shoulders. She tensed and made a move to shake him off, but he dropped his hands before it was necessary. "Are you all right? I mean, really?"

She shook her head. "*Nee*. I'm not all right. Is that what you came to hear? And what else? Were you hoping that I'd declare my love for you? You already know I love you. I promised myself to you years ago. But what does it matter? It means nothing now. Things are different. They will always be different, and you need to accept that. *I've* accepted it." She took a gasping breath, but she didn't falter in her stance.

"Have you?" he asked. "Have you really accepted it?"

Her shoulders dropped, and she regarded him through wide, teary eyes. Why was he pushing her? Why was he challenging her? He said he'd come to make sure she was all right, but with his very words, he was making everything worse.

"*Jah*," she stated, her voice strong. "I've accepted it."

"It's not too late…" he said, his voice soft. "I learned that in the *Englisch* world. It's never too late."

She stared at him, and something rose up inside of her. "That you can even stand there and say that to me, shows that you don't know me at all." Her words were clipped, angry.

"You're wrong," he said. "I *do* know you. I love you. I've always loved you, Maria."

"Go home," she said. "Please go home, Ike."

He looked as if he didn't believe her. As if he *couldn't* believe her. "Maria…" He moved toward her.

"Go home," she said again, barely able to draw breath. He needed to leave. Now. She couldn't bear another minute of this.

"All right. I'll go. This was a mistake." He gave her one long last look until she broke their gaze.

A wretched moment passed. She sucked in a tortured breath. He couldn't leave yet. Something burned in her—

something roared through her, and she had to know. She had to ask him. He was the only one she *could* ask.

"Ike?"

He turned back toward her. His eyes were flat, hard, wounded. "*Jah?*"

"If I had gone to an *Englisch* hospital, could they have saved my *boppli*?" Her voice was choked, her misery so acute, it was a physical pain.

Emotion flooded his face. His jaw tightened, and then he slowly shook his head. "*Ach*, Maria. My lovely, lovely Maria." He paused and drew in a long, agonized breath. "*Nee*. They couldn't have saved your *boppli*. It wouldn't have made any difference at all."

She clung to his words. She didn't know if he was telling the truth or trying to make her feel better. But either way, his saying so was his last gift to her. Her eyes welled with tears, and she took a small, faltering step back. He gazed at her for a long minute and then nodded and left her, standing in the middle of the pine trees, alone.

Chapter Twenty-Four

Mary hurried back. She felt wrung out, so exhausted, she could barely make it inside the house. Imagine Isaac coming all that way to see her. And he drove a car himself. She hadn't seen the car; she imagined he'd hidden it somewhere down the road. But…driving? He'd come to Hollybrook to take up his Amish life again. She assumed he was going to be baptized and join the church. Was she wrong? Was she assuming things about Isaac again, just as she had years before? Back then, she'd been sure he was going to be baptized and marry her right away. But instead, he'd disappeared into the *Englisch* world, leaving her bereft, not even knowing if he was safe or not.

If Bishop got wind of him driving again, Isaac was going to have trouble convincing him of his sincerity in being Amish.

She went straight upstairs to her room, not wanting to see Naomi. The astute older woman would guess something had happened out there on her walk, and Mary was in no frame of mind to share it with her.

Isaac had said it wouldn't have mattered if she'd seen

an *Englisch* doctor. Was it true? Would she have lost her *boppli* no matter how much doctoring she'd had?

She shut the door of her room and went to lie down on her bed. The worn quilt was soft beneath her cheek. It was cold up there so she was glad she hadn't removed her cape. She draped it more fully over her curled up body and closed her eyes. How different her life would be if she'd married Isaac. Everything would be different. Absolutely everything.

Her thoughts went to Mark. She'd never seen him look so forlorn as when she'd left. But she'd been certain she'd seen accusation in his eyes. He had said all the right things, and he'd tried to make her comfortable. But he had blamed her for losing the baby. He had. No matter what his lips had said, the blame had been there.

She squeezed her eyes more tightly shut. Could she fault him for it? She blamed herself, didn't she? Mark was right. It had been her fault.

But if what Isaac had said was true…

She shuddered and realized she was holding her breath. She purposefully took in a mouthful of air. *Rest now*, she thought. *Just rest.* She felt her chest loosen, and her muscles relax.

"Ike," she whispered into the empty room, "thank you for coming."

She imagined his face, his lopsided smile when he was really amused, and his hazel eyes crinkled up at the corners. She imagined the way he bent toward her when he was sharing something really exciting. The way his face lit up when he was curious. She imagined his easy stride, his way of moving through the world as if he hadn't a care.

"Good-bye," she murmured to his image. "Goodbye, dear, dear Ike."

Something cracked inside her and a rush of relief thundered through her with such power that she jerked on the bed. And then, just as quickly, it was gone. In its place lingered a tentative feeling of letting go.

Letting go…? Did that mean she didn't have to try anymore? She didn't have to fight? She didn't have to force herself to be any certain way? She didn't have to pretend anything?

Was it *really* over?

She blew out her breath in a sigh of release. *Over.* She pressed her hand over her lips. *Over.*

She turned onto her other side and fell into a deep sleep.

Mary slept through supper all the way until the next morning. When her eyes fluttered open and she looked about, she noticed the edges of morning creeping through her window. She was stunned. How was it possible to have slept so long? She got up and stretched, her muscles stiff and a bit achy. She was still in her clothes from the day before. If she hurried, she might be able to get in and out of the bathroom before Ezra or Naomi needed it. She snatched up some clean clothes and hurried down the hallway.

Minutes later, she stood beneath the shower and let the warm water run over her. She didn't want to stay in there too long and use up all of the gas-heated water, but it felt so good that she had a hard time rushing. The feeling she'd had the day before, that tenuous sensation of freedom, seemed to be holding. Mary was stunned and so grateful, tears ran down her face.

She was almost afraid to enjoy it. What if the feeling fled as quickly as it had come? She tested it by thinking of Isaac. She blinked. No yearning. No desperation. No regret.

Nothing but love—the kind she would have for any dear friend.

She sucked in her breath with awe. She purposefully thought of him again. The same. She began to laugh, a low chuckle deep in her throat.

And then she focused her mind on Mark. Her mood tightened and a wariness filled her. She had a lot of repair work to do where he was concerned, and she knew it. Deep in her soul, she knew it. She had no idea what she was going to do, but she did know that she wanted to fix things.

She rinsed the last remaining soap from her body and stepped out of the shower. She rubbed herself dry with the stiff, line-dried towel. She would start the day by writing him a letter. Her spirits lifted at the thought. Yes, she would write to him and attempt to begin the healing process between them. Would he accept her attempts? She had no idea.

She'd hurt him. Repeatedly. Not intentionally. No. He was her husband, and she had vowed before God to love him and care for him and be faithful to him. She fastened her apron over her dress. Had she? Had she been faithful to him?

Nausea rumbled in her stomach, and she clutched the edges of the sink. She closed her eyes and prayed…for wisdom and forgiveness and cleansing. For a new beginning. She placed her hands over her empty womb. A new beginning without her baby. She stiffened against the wave of grief.

Help me, help me, help me.

She picked up her nightgown and undergarments and headed back to her room. She gazed out the window, surprised that she hadn't heard Naomi stirring yet. The morning was well under way. She should probably go down and start breakfast, but she glanced at the notepad sitting on the bedside table. First, she would write to her husband.

Writing a letter before doing the chores went against everything she knew, everything she'd been taught, but she was going to do it anyway. She dropped her clothes on the end of her bed, picked up her pad and pen, and sank down on the mattress.

Dear Mark,
I am wondering how you're doing today. The sun is nigh up, and I shall have to go down and work on the morning meal, but I wanted to write to you first.
I miss you—

Mary paused. Did she? Her breath escaped in a quick burst. She did miss him. It felt so good to write those words and mean them…

I miss you and hope that you're doing well. It's getting so cold here, and I know Hollybrook is the same.
I am feeling better. I am healing.

She paused again. Would he care? Or was he so glad that she was gone that he hadn't given her a thought? Surely, he would want to know…

*I have been sewing. You know how I like to sew.
I'm thinking that when I return, I might make some
new curtains for the kitchen.*

   How are the livestock faring in the cold?

Mary cringed. What a stupid question. *How are the
livestock?* The livestock were perfectly well, and she
knew it. Why was it so hard to write to her own husband? She felt ridiculous writing such silliness. She
should tell him how she felt. That she was better. Truly
better. That she wanted them to love each other. She
wanted them to be married in every sense of the word.

But wasn't that what Mark had wanted all along? She
was the one who had blocked it. But shouldn't he know
that she'd changed her mind? Her heart? Shouldn't he
know that she loved him? Because she did.

And shouldn't he know that Isaac had come to see
her there in Linnow Creek?

She winced. Wasn't telling Mark about her talks with
Isaac what had caused this huge rift between them in the
first place? She should have kept her mouth shut. Yet,
that wasn't right either.

She tightened her grip on the pen. She wanted to tell
him that she was coming home, but she knew she wasn't
ready. She wanted to be ready, but she wasn't.

What if she looked into his eyes and only saw dis-
gust? Or hate? Or worse…indifference?

No. She couldn't face him. Not yet.

   I hope that you will want to write me back.
   Your wife,
   Mary

It was a pathetic ending to a pathetic letter. Mary stared at it. Was it better than not writing at all? She decided it was and folded it into an envelope. She affixed a stamp and slipped the letter beneath the waistband of her apron. She would run it out to the mailbox right away.

And then she would prepare the morning meal.

Chapter Twenty-Five

"A letter for you," Naomi called from the side door.

Mary set down the dress she was finishing and stood. She met Naomi in the hallway.

"Here you are," Naomi said.

Mary took the letter. When she saw that it was Deborah's handwriting, her heart fell. It had been four days since she'd written Mark. That was enough time for her letter to get to him and for him to respond.

"News from home, I expect," Naomi said.

Mary knew she was probing, wanting to know who had written. She looked at her aunt. "My friend," she said. "It's from my friend, Deborah."

"Not Mark then."

"*Nee*. Not Mark."

Naomi nodded, and Mary saw the concern in her eyes. Mary felt the same concern, but she didn't want to voice it.

"Is it time for you to be going home?"

Mary shriveled a little at her words.

Naomi reached out and touched her arm. "It ain't

that we don't want you here. It's been right nice. But I'm thinking your husband might be wanting you at home."

"I'm sure you're right, *Aenti*. But, but…maybe I can stay a few more days at least."

Naomi chuckled softly. "We're not tossing you out, my dear. Stay as long as you need."

"Thank you."

"Now, run off and read your letter."

Mary gave her a quick hug and went back into the sewing room. She sat in the rocker and opened Deborah's letter.

Dear Mary,
I have been thinking about you non-stop these days. How are you? Are you feeling better? My heart aches for you, Mary. Please come home. You need to be here with everyone who loves you.

Mark misses you. I know he does. Eli told me that Mark is walking around with his chin scraping the ground.

Come home. I'll help you all I can.

Mary stopped reading. Deborah help her? Deborah was the one with two little children and here she was offering help to her who had none. Shame burned through Mary's heart.

We're going to have a quilting frolic next week at Irma Yoder's place. I know how much you like to quilt. Wouldn't it be nice if you were back and we could go together?

I'm going to make fresh snickerdoodle cook-

ies this Friday. Please surprise me and be home
by then.
Your friend,
Deborah

Be home by then. Mary folded the letter and set it on
her lap. *Be home by then.* She glanced at the dark green
dress that was nearly finished. She only had a few more
minutes of work to do on the hem. Would Naomi have
another project for her after that?

Mary picked up the dress and took up the needle.
She pushed it through the fabric in neat, tiny stitches.
She secretly prided herself on the fact that no hem she'd
sewn had ever come loose. Not once. She continued
sewing, pushing the needle in and out. The rhythm of
it soothed her.

So…a quilting frolic at Irma's. Mary was known for
her skill at quilting. If she wasn't there… Of course,
everyone surely knew she was away at Linnow Creek,
but they would be wondering when she was going to return. It had been some days now—in truth, longer than
she'd planned to be gone when she'd fled. Not that she
had thought it through at the time. All she'd wanted to
do was escape.

And now? What did she want?

She wanted Mark to write to her. She wanted him to
want her back home.

Maybe he had written and his letter had gotten lost. It
did happen sometimes. She remembered when the round
robin letter circulating through her extended family had
gotten lost between her mother's second cousin and her.
It had been a mystery until one day it had shown up in

the mailbox, definitely worse for the wear—dirty and
crumpled and the address hardly legible.

But Mary's family had rejoiced in it all the same.

So yes, letters did get delayed.

Mary finished the hem and bit off the thread. Who
was she kidding? Mark hadn't written to her. His letter wasn't lost in the corner of a post office somewhere.
He hadn't written.

Plain and simple.

The evening meal was subdued. Mary's mind was
full, and she couldn't bring herself to be much of a con-
versationalist. Both Naomi and Ezra seemed to sense
this, and they ate quietly. Ezra commented now and
again on the tasty food, but other than that, it was silent.

"I'll *red* up the kitchen," Mary said when the meal
was over.

"I'll help you, child," Naomi said.

Mary stood and picked up her dirty dishes. "*Nee.*
I'd like to do it myself. Why don't you go into the front
room and relax a bit?"

Naomi gave her an appreciative smile. "I won't argue
with that."

"Come, wife," Ezra said. "Let's read a while."

Mary toted the dishes to the kitchen. She squirted
some soap into the sink and ran the tap. The warm water
felt good on her hands. She scrubbed the dishes, setting
them in the drainer to dry. She could hear the hum of
Naomi's and Ezra's voices carry in from the other room.
Such a comforting sound. She wondered if she and Mark
would ever be that compatible and comfortable with each
other. Her aunt and uncle must have been married going

on forty years now. How wonderful to be connected to someone for so long.

She put the last dish in the drainer and wiped her hands on the towel, tossing it back onto the counter. She looked around, thinking she should prepare for breakfast. But first, she wanted to take a walk. She leaned over the sink, peering out into the dark night. It was hard to tell just how cold it was out there, but she saw edges of ice forming on the outside of the window.

No matter. She needed to be outside. Needed to look up at the sky. Needed to feel the air on her face.

"I'm going for a short walk," she said, poking her head into the front room.

"*Ach!* Mary, it's freezing out there," Ezra pointed out.

"Let her go, Ezra. She'll come in if she gets too cold." Naomi patted his knee.

"I'll be in shortly," Mary said and left. She bundled up carefully in her cape. She wrapped her scarf around her neck numerous times and put on her mittens. Her thick shoes were enough to stave off the cold. Plus, she'd put on long stockings that morning, which always helped.

As soon as she opened the door, the cold affronted her. She braced herself against it and stepped out onto the grass. She walked to the center of the yard and stood very still. She could already feel her nose growing pink with the cold. The only sounds were the gentle rustling of the few dead leaves clinging to the branches above her. Looking up, she saw the stars hanging like crisp lanterns speckling the sky.

Why did everything seem so much quieter in the cold? In the moonlight, she saw her breath making puffs of white that dissipated immediately into nothing—as if the breath had never been breathed in the first place.

Her baby had never drawn breath.

Mary pressed against her hollow womb. Tears burned her eyes, but she blinked them away.

"Is my little one with you, *Gott*? Is my little one safe?" Mary whispered into the sky. "I miss my *boppli*. I miss my *boppli* so much."

She sucked in a gulping sob and felt the sting of the cold on her throat.

"I need to go home, don't I?" she continued. "I need to go home."

She walked to the thick tree beside her and leaned against its rough bark. She looked out in front of her... seeing the house with its faint light leaking through the windows, seeing the smoke billowing up from the chimney, seeing the expanse of the fallow fields stretching out behind the house in shadowed darkness.

She heard a muffled neigh from the barn. Most of the livestock would be sleeping by now, the hens would be perched in their nesting boxes for the night. Mary cocked her head toward the barn but heard nothing further. If she focused her gaze far beyond the property, she could see the glow of an electric street light and how it smudged the sky with a yellow haze.

It was peaceful out there. Calm. She drew in a long slow breath.

Tomorrow, she thought. Tomorrow, she'd make arrangements for a van to take her back home. She wondered if she should write Mark and tell him she was coming, but she decided against it. She would just go home.

Where she belonged.

Chapter Twenty-Six

Mary was the first one down the next morning. She had made a good start on the pancake batter when Naomi came in.

"*Ach*, girl, you're putting me to shame."

Mary laughed. "Nonsense. You always are the first one down here. It's about time I returned the favor."

"Pancakes?"

"*Jah*. And I've got some left-over potatoes from yesterday's noon meal to fry up."

"I'll get the slabs of bacon out." Naomi yawned and went to the fridge for the bacon. She set the meat on the counter and reached into the drawer beneath the oven to pull out a cast iron skillet. "Ezra will be going out to the animals in a minute, and he'll be ready for something hot when he gets back."

"I've got the coffee started."

"How was your walk last night?"

"I'm going home," Mary said quietly.

Naomi stepped close and touched her shoulder. "That's *gut*. That's real *gut*."

"I'll need to hire a driver and van."

"*Jah*, you will. We can call Aaron Benson from the phone shanty."

"Does he live here in Linnow Creek?"

"He does," Naomi said. "Most all of us Amish folk use him for transportation. He'll take you right away if he's not busy. You may have to wait a day or two, though."

Mary sighed. "I guess that can't be helped."

"Does Mark know you're coming?"

"*Nee.*" She looked at her aunt. "But he will when I get there."

Naomi chuckled. "That's for sure and for certain."

Finished making the batter, Mary grabbed a second skillet from under the oven. "I won't start these until Ezra gets back in. Otherwise, they kind of turn rubbery."

"He'd appreciate that," Naomi said as she arranged the strips of bacon into the pan. "But I can get these cooked right away. I was thinking of fried chicken for the noon meal. Does that suit?"

"That suits just fine," Mary said, knowing she was going to miss her aunt when she returned home.

By mid-morning, most of the chores were finished, and Mary was ready to run down the road to the phone shanty to call Aaron Benson. Naomi had written out the number for her and told her exactly where the shanty was.

She put on her cape, scarf, and mittens and headed outside. She walked quickly, not taking much time to enjoy the frozen scenery. She hadn't gone far, when she spotted the shanty just ahead, a few yards off the road.

Inside, it was almost as cold as outside. She picked up the receiver and dialed the number.

"Hello?" answered a male voice.

"Hello. Is this Aaron Benson?"

"It is. In the flesh. How can I help you?"

"My name is Mary Schrock. I need a ride to Holly-brook as soon as possible."

"Hmm. Hollybrook, huh? Is it an emergency?"

Was it? To her, perhaps, but not really.

"*Nee*."

"I am committed until tomorrow afternoon. Will that be soon enough?"

"*Jah*." Longer than she would have liked, but still, tomorrow afternoon wasn't that far away.

"Where are you?"

"I'm staying with my *aenti*, Naomi, and my *onkel*, Ezra—"

"Oh, I know them," Aaron interrupted. "I'll be there around two-thirty. I'll have you back in Hollybrook by suppertime."

"Thank you. I'll be ready. Good-bye," she said and hung up.

On her way back to the house, she tried to imagine Mark's face when she showed up. She prayed it would reflect pleasure. *I'm coming, Mark*, she thought. *I'm coming home*.

When she got back to the house, she told Naomi of her plans and then went upstairs to pack what she could. It would only take her a few minutes as she hadn't brought much, but it would make her feel better to get ready.

Chapter Twenty-Seven

Mary sat on the bed looking at her half-packed suitcase. This was going to be a long day, she thought. A very, very long day.

Maybe she should take advantage of the time and visit her cousins. She'd seen them a few times since she'd come, but basically only at church service. Yet, perhaps her time would be better spent helping Naomi with something. She'd never be able to repay her aunt for her kindness and generosity.

She was ready to go downstairs when she heard gravel crunch on the drive outside. Had Aaron been able to come earlier after all? She flew to the window and pulled the curtains aside. Her heart lurched to her throat when she saw the van stop and Mark get out.

Mark? What was he doing there?

She let the curtains fall and stood still, as if frozen. She heard the van door shut and the front door of the house open. Muffled voices rose to her, Naomi greeting Mark, Mark's low voice in response. Instinctively, her hands went to her hair, smoothing it, making sure it was tidy under her *kapp*. She swallowed and forced herself to breathe.

Had he come for her? Was he there to take her home? Had he missed her? Why else would he have come?

She sucked in a huge gulp of air, straightened her shoulders, and went downstairs.

He was standing in the front room when she entered. His blue eyes were darker than normal, shadowed, cautious. His blond hair had been recently cut—who had done that? He still wore his heavy winter coat, and he still wore his shoes that were making slow puddles of dirty water on Naomi's pristine floor.

"Mark," Mary uttered, her voice breathy. Her lungs had constricted, making breathing nearly impossible. Every muscle was taut. Standing there before him, she actually hurt. His eyes met hers and held. She tried to read the emotion there, but she couldn't do it. He was wary of her, that was clear. Was he glad to see her? She saw his jaw tense, saw the tightness of his shoulders even beneath his coat.

"Hello, Mary." His deep voice nearly made her weep. She hadn't realized how much she'd missed hearing him. He made no move to come to her.

Naomi stepped to Mark. "Give me your coat, son. It's right warm in here." She turned to Mary. "Isn't it nice that your husband has come?"

Mary nodded, not trusting herself to speak without bursting into tears.

Mark shrugged out of his coat and let Naomi take it. Only then did he seem to realize he had tromped mud into the house.

"*Ach*, Naomi, my boots. I'm sorry."

Naomi fluttered her hand at him. "Mud can be mopped. Don't you worry about it."

He was already bending over to remove them. He took the boots back to the front door and set them on a rubber mat. "Do you have a rag? I can clean up my mess."

Naomi laughed. "Goodness! I can clean my own floors, for sure and for certain. You sit down and visit with your wife."

Mark turned back to Mary, his brows raised. Mary nearly stumbled on her way to sit on the davenport. She perched close to the middle, hoping he would sit beside her. He didn't. He crossed over to a rocker and sat down.

Naomi had taken Mark's coat to the wash room. She was back now with a rag, and she made quick work of the puddles. "Mary, I need to go into town to pick up some more lard and baking soda. I'll be back shortly."

Mary knew full well that Naomi did not need more lard. She already had a tubful in the cabinet next to the cook stove. But she appreciated her intent. She and Mark would have the house to themselves with no one around to overhear their conversation.

"Thank you, *Aenti*," she said.

When she heard the side door shut, she turned to Mark. "You came."

"I came," he repeated. He rubbed his hands over his thighs, back and forth, as if they were paining him.

"I had already called for a van," she said softly, watching for his reaction. "He was coming for me tomorrow."

"To take you back to Hollybrook?"

Well, where else would she be going? she wondered. "*Jah*. Of course."

He raised his head slightly, as if digesting the news. "I didn't know if you were coming back at all."

"Mark! Of course, I was coming back. I told you that."

He cocked his head to the side. "Maybe."

She frowned. "Maybe? You really thought I might not return?"

He gripped the arms of the rocker. "Mary, I don't even know you anymore. I haven't the slightest idea what you might do or where you might go."

She flinched, feeling as if he'd struck her. Had it really gotten that bad?

"I always intended to come home," she said slowly. She licked her lips. "I was coming tomorrow."

"Then, I guess I wasted the trip."

Her brow creased. "*Nee.* I'm glad you came." The words rushed from her mouth.

He looked surprised, but he didn't say anything.

"I want to go home."

"That's something, then," he said finally. "The van is picking me up in an hour. I made arrangements."

"So, I'll go with you?" she asked.

"Do you want to?"

Frustration heaved through her. "*Jah.*" Hadn't she made herself clear?

Mark gazed around the room. "I forgot what a nice place this is."

So, he wanted to change the subject? She sank back into the cushion. "I made a dress for Naomi."

He looked at her. "That's nice."

"Isaac came to see me," she blurted and then nearly gagged. What had possessed her to utter that?

The effect of her words was instantaneous. Mark exploded up from the rocker and glared at her. *"What?"*

She cringed at the anger on his face. She shrank back

into the davenport, wanting to draw her knees up to her chest. Instead, she circled her waist with her arms.

"He came *here*?" Mark thundered. He hovered over her like a bull. *"Why?"*

Mary blinked rapidly, squishing herself even farther into the cushion.

"And how did he know you were here? Did you *tell him*?" His words pelted her.

"Nee!" she cried back. "I don't know how he knew! I only know he came!"

"Into this house?"

"Nee. He met me out on the road."

"He *met* you? On the *road*?" Mark's voice was dipped in acid.

"I didn't know he was there!" she cried, tears pouring down her face. "I wouldn't have gone out if I'd known."

Was that true? Wouldn't she have gone out? She pressed her hands over her mouth and tried to stifle her own sobs.

Mark leaned down. "What did you do with him?"

"Nothing! We talked. I sent him away." She was nearly blubbering now, and she hated the sound of it.

He straightened then. "You sent him away?"

"Jah! I sent him away. I *did.*" Mary wiped at her cheeks. "I don't want to see him anymore. I *don't* want to see him anymore."

Mark exhaled with a quick blast of air. "Why not? Why don't you?"

And then she saw it. His despair. His vulnerability. His pain. She saw it in the sudden slump of his shoulders, the twitch at the side of his mouth. The darkening of his eyes. The way his brows creased low on his forehead.

She wanted to go to him. Press herself against him.

Put her arms around him. Bury herself in him. But she was afraid…afraid if she moved, he'd bolt. And then, he'd be gone from her forever.

She put her hands on her lap and looked at him. "I don't want to see him because it makes you unhappy. Because it's over between Isaac and me, and has been over for years. And because I love you."

A muscle next to his eye contracted.

He stared at her, as if trying to read her soul. As if trying to discern whether she was telling the truth.

She held her breath.

He sighed and stepped to the davenport and sat down. Still, he didn't say a word. Nor did he look at her.

"I'm sorry," she whispered. "For everything."

He didn't respond. He continued to stare down at the floor.

"And I shouldn't have gone outside to fetch the eggs." Her voice faltered, but she forced herself to continue. "I know you're angry with me about that. Maybe, you even hate me." Again, she stifled a sob. "I will never forgive myself for it. Never."

She saw that his eyes had filled with tears. She wanted to take him in her arms, but she was still afraid. She had destroyed so much between them, and she didn't know if it was too late to get any of it back.

But he *had* come to Linnow Creek. That had to mean something. It just *had* to.

"Mark?" she whispered.

He shook his head slowly, over and over again, still not looking at her. "It's useless," he muttered. "Useless."

Panic roared through her. "*Nee!* It isn't. Mark, *it isn't.*" She touched his leg, and he flinched. She drew back her hand as if burned.

They sat there, both of them, frozen in their own misery. Finally, Mary couldn't stand the silence another minute.

"*Gott* will help us," she murmured. "He will."

Mark turned his face toward her. His eyes were red and full of tears. "Will he?"

Mary gasped. Didn't he believe anymore? "*Jah*. He will."

Mark jerked up off the davenport and faced her. "I have been praying for him to help me for a long time, Mary. So far, I haven't seen a lot."

She gaped at him. Their months together played out in her mind. Mark used to be lighter, more positive. Happy. He used to make her laugh. Granted, not as much as Isaac had… She clenched her hands, twisting them together until they hurt. She was not going to compare Mark to Isaac. She was done with that. She stood and stepped closer.

"It's going to be all right, now," she said, praying that her words were true. "I'm sorry. I'm going to make it up to you."

He gazed down at her. Somewhere in his look of despair, she thought she saw a flicker of hope. She latched onto it.

"We're going to be all right, Mark. If you'll let me go home with you…"

His eyes searched her face, settling on her lips. She burned inside—burned with the need to be wanted, burned with the desire to make everything up to him, burned with the yearning for both of them to be happy again.

She stood motionless and waited. With a sudden movement, he pulled her roughly to him. She felt her knees weaken as his mouth descended upon hers. His lips were hard and searching, and she succumbed to the domination of his kiss. She lost herself in him then, in his passion and need. When they finally broke apart, her entire body tingled, and she had difficulty standing.

"Come home," he choked out, his voice gruff and heavy.

With a gasp of relief, she pressed herself against his chest, feeling the quick beat of his heart and the tension in his muscles. He was still hesitant toward her—she felt it rumbling through him.

She wasn't a fool.

There was so much still to be said. So much still to be worked through. For her. And him. And the two of them together.

But this was a start, wasn't it? She was going home. She squeezed her eyes shut and tightened her grip on him. If they were together, they had a chance. A chance to rebuild their life. A chance to be happy again.

"Mark?" she murmured.

"Mmm-hmm?" He buried his lips in her *kapp*.

"Thank you." She drew back and looked into his dear face. She blinked back her tears. "Can we go home now?"

He nodded. "We can go home."

When she tried to pull away to go upstairs and pack the rest of her things, he wouldn't let her go. She laughed softly.

"Come upstairs with me?" she murmured.

"*Jah*," he answered. He put his arm around her shoulders, and together, they climbed the stairs to the bedroom.

Chapter Twenty-Eight

$\backsim$

Back in Hollybrook, Mary stood inside her bedroom and stared at the bed. The wedding-pattern quilt her mother had pieced together for her lay flat and clean across the mattress. So clean, in fact, that no one would ever guess it had recently been drenched in blood.

"How did you—?" Mary couldn't finish her question to her husband. A sharp pain ripped through her stomach, nearly bending her double. *Nee. Not again.* Her hand tightened its grip around the suitcase handle, and she shoved the pain aside. A memory. That was all it was. A memory.

She didn't hurt anymore. At least, not her stomach. Not her womb.

Mark pried the suitcase from her hand. "Your *mamm*," he said quietly. "She took the quilt home after... I don't know how she got it clean, but she did." He searched her face. "Are you pleased?"

Mary swallowed hard and nodded. "*Jah*," she answered. She forced more energy into her voice. "*Jah*. I'm right pleased. Thank you, Mark."

"Do you need some time to unpack? Supper is in the refrigerator. It just needs warmed."

"Did you cook it?" Mary asked, surprised.

"*Nee*, 'twas your *mamm*. And Deborah. They brought food over."

Mary dipped her head. "I see. It won't take much for me to unpack. I wasn't at *Aenti's* for long."

"Nearly a month, Mary. Long enough."

Her gaze flew to his. Searching, always searching. Scrutinizing his face, trying to detect his mood. His frame of mind. Wondering whether he was still angry with her. About the miscarriage. About Isaac. About the total mess she'd made of things. But he had turned away from her, and she couldn't see his face.

"I'll be down shortly," she said. "And I'll warm up the food. No need for you to worry yourself over it."

She could hardly imagine Mark in the kitchen anyway. It wasn't proper for a man to be fussing with food. While she'd been gone, she knew Mark must have fixed his own meals. Or maybe, her mother had invited him over. Still, it would hardly have happened every day or for every meal. Right after Mary had miscarried—before she'd fled to her aunt's—Mark had fixed her a meal or two. Not that she'd eaten much during those days.

Mary placed her suitcase on the bed. Those days were over. She had returned, and she was determined to put their lives back together. Determined to take this second chance and build something good, something true and loving and joyful.

Joyful? Perhaps that was taking it too far. Or perhaps not. They served a mighty God, didn't they?

Mary unpacked her few belongings and tucked most of them into the dresser drawers. She hung her dresses on two of the pegs that ran around the walls. She picked up the hand mirror from the top of the dresser and looked at herself. The brown circles under her dark eyes were almost totally gone. Her cheeks still looked a bit sunken, but not as bad as they had been before. If she could get back to her old routine and eating, she'd look normal again before long.

She heard the oven door slam shut. Had Mark started to cook even after she'd asked him not to? She took a deep breath, smoothed her apron, and went downstairs. She walked into the kitchen and stopped short.

"*Mamm!*"

Sandra Hochstetler turned from the cook stove. She crossed the room to Mary and embraced her with a quick hug. "*Ach*, Mary. You're finally back."

"I didn't hear you come in."

"Your father dropped me off at the road. He needed the pony cart for an errand, but he'll be back to fetch me later."

"You didn't have to come. I can fix the meal just fine."

Sandra's eyes were soft on hers. "It's wonderful *gut* to see you. Are you well? How were my sister and her husband? Did you see your cousins?"

"Goodness, *Mamm*. One question at a time."

Sandra's hands flew up. "You're right. You're right. You've hardly had time to catch your breath." She put a hand to Mary's cheek. "You look tired."

"It was a long journey," Mary said, even though it hadn't taken the Mennonite driver much more than two hours to deliver her and Mark to Hollybrook.

"Of course, it was. You sit down here by the warming stove and tell me all about it."

"I'd rather get supper on the table. I told Mark I would."

"Mark knows I'm here. He isn't going to care as long as the meal gets to the table."

Mark might not care, but Mary did. She was determined to put things right as soon as possible, and even though she appreciated her mother's help, she didn't need it.

"How about *you* sit down for a bit and tell me about my *dat* and my brothers. And whatever else I missed around here," Mary said, taking the fork her mother had just picked up.

"You're downright bossy, daughter, you know that?" Sandra said, but she was laughing.

"Bossy it is, then," Mary responded. She turned to the bowl and began cutting the lard into the flour mixture. "Biscuits, I'm thinking."

"*Jah*, biscuits. I know how Mark loves them."

Mary smiled. "That he does."

"So, my sister was fine?"

"*Jah*. She and Ezra were real kind to me."

"You knew they would be."

Mary paused. "*Jah*, I knew they would be."

Sandra came over to stand by her again. "The main thing is you're feeling better, and you're back in your own home. I'm right glad, daughter."

"Thank you." Mary began working the dough again. "And thank you for...well, for getting my quilt clean again."

"It weren't nothing. I did have to replace a few pieces here and there, but I thought it came out fine."

"It looks beautiful. Just like when you first gave it to Mark and me."

The two of them worked together to get the meal on the table. Sandra refused to set a place for herself, insisting that Mary's father would be back for her before the meal began. And she was right. Zeb came rolling up to the porch in the pony cart just as Mary put the last dish on the table.

Mark came in from the front room. "Why don't the both of you stay and eat?" he asked her mother.

Sandra shook her head. "My boys will be waiting for me. Thanks kindly, anyway." She gave Mary a tender look. "I'll be seeing you soon, dear," she said and scurried out the door.

As soon as Sandra was gone, a terrible silence descended on the house. Mary stood awkwardly for a moment, and then she walked to the table.

"It's ready," she told Mark.

"Smells right *gut*," he said stiffly and took his seat.

Mary sat down, too, and then Mark bowed his head. "Shall we pray?"

Mary closed her eyes and pleaded with God for wisdom and grace. She pleaded with him that this meal would be pleasant. She asked that conversation would flow easily and that the pervasive sense of discomfort hovering over them would go away. She'd hoped this awkwardness would be gone. She'd harbored real hope of it back at her aunt's house. But it had descended quickly enough, once they'd stepped foot back in their own house.

Mark cleared his throat, and the silent blessing was over.

"Would you pass me the potatoes, please," Mark asked, holding out his hand.

"Gladly," she answered and handed him the heavy

glass bowl. She scooted the rest of the food toward his plate, and then she helped herself.

"It's *gut* to see you eating again, Mary."

She nodded and took a bite of green beans.

"I'll be heading up north a piece with Eli tomorrow."

Mary raised her brow. "With Deborah's husband?"

"*Jah*. He wants to look at a plow that's for sale. It ain't far, so we'll be taking a buggy."

"Maybe I'll pop over to see Deborah and the *kinner* then. I'm eager to catch up on the news."

"I'll take you over there with me when I go. We'll be using Eli's buggy, though, for the trip."

Mary wasn't surprised. When Deborah and Eli had purchased their new buggy the year before, Deborah had been right pleased, telling Mary how much more comfortable the seats were than those in their previous buggy. Mary hadn't yet had an opportunity to try them out, but she was glad Mark would get the chance.

"Will you be gone all day?" she asked.

"I doubt it. But you never know."

That was true. Sometimes, it took a while if there were a lot of *Englisch* cars on the road.

"If Eli decides on the plow, how will he get it to his farm?" Mary asked.

Mark took a piece of bread from his plate and slathered a thick layer of fresh butter on it. "Don't rightly know. I reckon he has some idea in mind."

Mary finished eating her helping of potatoes. She was looking forward to the next day. She was eager to visit Deborah, not having seen her for some weeks now. Deborah's tiny babe and her little toddler had both probably grown quite a little while she was gone.

"It's *gut* to be back," Mary said, glancing at Mark.

He swallowed his mouthful and reached over to take her hand. "It's *gut* to have you back."

There was so much left unsaid between them. Mary looked into the deep blue eyes of her husband and yearned to see him smile. Yearned to see him happy again. But she was back now, and living together again was the first step.

"I need to tend to a few things in the barn," Mark told her. "I'll be out there for a while."

"All right," she answered, disliking the formality of his words.

He finished up his meal and stood. He licked his lips and for a moment, he looked uncertain. Mary stood quickly and stepped close. She put a hand on his arm. He went stiff and looked down into her eyes. Her heart hammered against her ribs. Doing her best to fight the fear that gripped her, she stood on her tiptoes and kissed her husband's cheek.

"Stay warm out there," she whispered.

Mark didn't move. He seemed frozen in place. Mary sank back onto her feet. She wished she knew what he was thinking. She didn't even know whether her physical gestures of affection were welcome. But when she saw the expression in his eyes, her heart went cold.

There it was. His doubt. His disbelief.

He didn't trust her. She drew in a long breath. *He didn't trust her.* She squared her shoulders. Not yet, but he would. She would make certain of that.

"I'll see you when you get back in," she said softly.

He seemed to shake himself out of his stupor. "*Jah. Jah.* Of course." He left the room so quickly, Mary half expected a gale of wind in his wake. The side door slammed closed, and he was gone.

Chapter Twenty-Nine

Mary took her time cleaning up after the meal. It was good to be back in her own kitchen with her own things. Some of the dishes had been put back in the wrong spots, but she corrected that quickly. When she was finished, she looked about the simple space with satisfaction. She glanced toward the staircase, knowing what she must do. She wiped her hands on the dishtowel, hanging it carefully on its hook at the end of the counter. She'd have to face it sometime, and it might as well be now…

She braced herself, picked up one of the lit lanterns, and walked to the stairs, climbing them slowly, deliberately. Once in the upstairs hallway, she moved to the bedroom across from hers and Mark's. She pushed open the door and stepped inside. The lantern threw a yellow circle of light over the room, and her gaze immediately went to the far wall. She sucked in her breath.

It was gone. As if it had never been there in the first place.

Mark must have rearranged the furniture. The space where the cradle had been was now taken up with a small bench. She walked over to it and sat down.

Her eyes welled with tears, and she let herself cry, the tears gently coursing down her cheeks. The cradle for their baby had been beautiful—a labor of love and hope crafted in secret. She remembered when she'd seen it for the first time, and that she had wept, just as she was doing now in its absence. It hadn't been that long ago that she had nestled it beneath the window in that very room.

Now, it seemed a lifetime ago.

Where had he put it? Back in the barn loft where he'd made it? She sat stiffly, her back erect and her hands on her lap. Would they need it again? Would there ever be a little baby sleeping in it with its little hands curled beneath its chin?

Old Mae had told her there would be plenty of other babies. Mary supposed the old medicine woman was right. But at that moment, she couldn't muster up much confidence.

She shuddered. No matter. God's will would be done. She stood and wiped her tears away. Enough. She'd let herself cry, but now, it was enough. She walked across the hall to her bedroom. Even with the lantern, the corners of the room were shrouded in shadows. Mary went to the bed and turned down the covers on both sides. She hadn't shared a bed with Mark for a long time. Would he come up to the room with her tonight?

Or would he stay in one of the other bedrooms? It was still early, but she was tired and on edge. She set the lantern on the bedside table and undressed, pulling on her nightgown. She grabbed a shawl from its peg on the wall and wrapped it about her shoulders. Mark would be surprised that she was already dressed for bed.

She heard the side door in the wash room downstairs

close. He was back inside. She wasn't sure whether to go back down and sit with him for a while in front of the warming stove, or stay put and wait for him to come upstairs. She didn't have to ponder long, for she heard his footsteps on the stairs. She sank to the edge of the bed.

He came to the door, his tall shadow looming. "Mary?"

"I was tired," she said.

"Not too surprising," he said and walked to the bed. He stood above her, staring down into her face. He reached out and touched her hair, now loose from its *kapp*.

"I always liked your hair," he said softly. "It has a pretty wave to it."

She blinked up at him. She bit her lower lip to keep it from trembling and held her breath. He sank down on the bed beside her, the mattress dipping. She leaned against him and felt the muscles in his arms tense.

"Morning will come early," he said stiffly.

She blinked, and disappointment swept through her. "*Jah*. Morning will come early."

He stood and with his back to her, he took off his clothes and pulled on his nightwear. He looked over his shoulder at her. Their eyes locked and neither said a word. The moment stretched and then fell flat. Mary looked down at her hands.

"Where did you put the cradle?" she asked.

"The barn." There was a hitch in his voice.

She shifted and got under the covers, tugging the quilt over her. "I see."

Mark moved to the other side of the bed and climbed in. He situated himself and then lay still. "We'll need it again…" he told her. "The cradle. Someday."

Mary exhaled and closed her eyes, relief flooding her. "Someday," she repeated, her voice soft.

Mary climbed into the pony cart next to Mark. The air was frigid, and both of them were heavily bundled.

"I don't know when Eli and I will be back," Mark told her as he guided Flame onto the main road. "Will you be all right at Deborah's the full day if necessary?"

"*Jah*. We have a lot to catch up on. I'm sure she could use a hand with her chores, too."

"All right." Mark fell silent, his hands resting on his knees as he held the reins.

Mary blinked against the cold and gazed out over the empty fields. There was something lonely about fields already put away for the winter. Frequent smatterings of trees dotted the landscape, breaking the monotony with their naked branches like silent silhouettes against the sky.

Mary settled in for the short drive. It didn't take long to arrive at Deborah's, and Mary was glad to get inside the warm house.

"Mary!" Deborah cried, rushing to her while balancing the baby on her hip. "It's right *gut* to see you."

Mary gave her a hug and then drew back to tickle Rachel under the chin. The baby gurgled and looked at Mary with wide blue eyes.

"Land's sake, but she's grown."

Deborah nodded. "That she has." She glanced around. "Ross! Ross, where are you? Mary's come to visit."

There was a pattering of little feet as Ross came running in from the kitchen. He stopped short when he saw Mary and promptly stuck two fingers in his mouth.

"Hello, Ross. How are you?"

He didn't answer; instead, he vigorously sucked his fingers. Mary laughed.

Deborah's husband, Eli, came in from the wash room bringing the outside cold with him. "Mark's here, so we're off," he told Deborah. He glanced at Mary and nodded. "We'll be back as soon as I see that plow."

"You going to buy it?" Deborah asked.

"Don't rightly know. Have to see it first." He leaned forward and kissed Deborah on the cheek. He ran his hand over Rachel's head, and tousled Ross's hair. "You two be *gut* for your *mamm*."

And he was gone. Mark had stayed outside, taking care of Flame and the cart. Mary moved to the window and saw him climb into Eli's buggy.

"I've got tea on," Deborah said. "Come on through."

Mary pulled away from the window and followed Deborah into the kitchen. The kettle was whistling, and Deborah proceeded to make tea.

"You sure can do a lot while still holding the *boppli*," Mary observed.

Deborah laughed. "Practice. You'll learn how to do the same soon enough." And then she paused, her face wrinkling with concern. "*Ach*, I'm sorry. Me and my big mouth. Forgive me."

"There's nothing to forgive," Mary assured her, ignoring the familiar zap of pain rushing through her. "It's over and done now."

Deborah poured the steaming water. "You'll have others. Lots and lots of others."

Mary nodded. "That's what Old Mae told me…"

"Then, it must be true. She would know if it were otherwise. She's the one who took care of you…afterward…"

"I know. Everything will be fine. As the Lord *Gott* wills."

They sat at the table with their tea. Ross had trundled into the kitchen behind them and was now playing with wooden blocks on the floor. Baby Rachel seemed content to sit on Deborah's lap.

"Your time with your *aenti* was worthwhile?"

"I had to go, Deborah. I had to get out of here at least for a while. And it helped. I'm better."

"And Mark…?"

Mary nodded resolutely. "He's better, too. Truth be told, it's a bit awkward between us, but it's going to be fine. Truly."

"I don't doubt that," Deborah was quick to assure her. She took a sip of the steaming liquid. "Isaac wasn't at service last Sunday."

Mary stiffened. "It's nothing to me."

Deborah reached out and touched her hand. "I know it isn't. I'm sorry. I can't think why I even mentioned it."

"He's dead to me now. He has to be." Mary fingered the handle on her cup. "He came to see me in Linnow Creek."

Deborah let out a soft gasp. *"What?"*

"He did. I told him to go away."

"Did he leave?"

Mary glanced at her. "Of course, he did."

"Does Mark know."

"*Jah*. Mark knows."

"And…?"

"He knows I sent Isaac away."

Deborah looked relieved. "*Gut*."

"Do you think he's still around the area?" Mary asked.

"I'm sure he is. I would have heard otherwise. But if you sent him away, he shouldn't be bothering you again."

Bothering her? Is that what Isaac had been doing? She supposed it was. Of *course*, it was, she admonished herself. Of course, that was what he'd been doing. But still, she'd been glad for her contact with him. She now *felt* like it was over, not just knew in her head that it was. Feeling it helped. It helped a lot.

"I have a huge pile of ironing… I remember that you helped me with it once before."

Mary laughed. "And I'll be happy to help you with it again. As soon as we finish our tea, I'll get right on it."

"You're a *gut* friend, Mary Schrock. I only wish I could have helped you more when, well, you know."

"Just knowing you were here was a comfort to me." Mary drank her tea more quickly now, eager to stop this line of conversation and get to work.

Deborah seemed to sense her mood, and she gulped down the rest of her tea as well. Mary carried both empty cups to the sink. "Shall we get started on the ironing?"

"I'm not going to say *nee* to that." Deborah handed Mary the baby and set up the ironing board next to the warming stove. She already had two heavy irons heating on the surface of the stove.

Rachel stirred and started to fuss in Mary's arms. Mary held her close and cooed over her. Rachel stopped fussing and settled in, closing her eyes again. The baby felt good in Mary's arms. Soft and sweet and vulnerable. Mary breathed her in, enjoying her fresh baby scent even as it was tinged with the slightly sour smell of spit-up. With a laugh, Mary snuggled the child closer.

Deborah stood next to the ironing board, regarding Mary. "You look right natural holding that *boppli*, Mary.

My prediction is that by this time next year, you'll be holding your own sweet babe."

Mary blinked back her tears and smiled at her friend. "The Lord *Gott* willing…"

"The Lord *Gott* is willing," Deborah said firmly. "It's the way of things, isn't it?"

Yes, it was the way of things.

Chapter Thirty

The ironing had been finished up hours ago. The two women had tended the children, baked bread, and prepared both the noon meal, which they had eaten, and the evening meal. Now, they sat at the table, staring at the supper. Darkness had fallen outside, as it always fell so early during the winter months.

"I thought they'd be back by now," Deborah said.

Mary glanced through the window. "*Jah*. So did I."

"I don't like it when Eli drives the buggy in the dark."

"He has lanterns he hangs out, doesn't he?"

"*Jah*. But still. That light is awful feeble compared to them lights on cars. I just don't like it."

"They'll be back real soon, I'm sure." Mary looked at the table full of food. "In the meantime, we might as well eat. Afterward, we can keep the food warm for the men."

Deborah shook herself out of her daze. "You're right. Let's eat, and then we can get the *kinner* to bed."

They ate quietly, except for Ross, who seemed to delight in throwing his food off the tray and then pointing at it and squealing with glee. When the meal was over, Mary held Rachel while Deborah went to put Ross to bed. She came down the stairs about fifteen minutes later, looking exhausted. "The men back yet?"

Mary shook her head. Deborah sighed and took the baby. "I'm getting real tense, Mary. I don't like this at all." She looked down and nuzzled Rachel's head. "I'll run back upstairs and put this little one down."

"Take your time," Mary called after her.

Within minutes, Deborah was back downstairs. "I can't imagine what's taking them so long."

"They'll be here any minute. Maybe Eli bought the plow, and it took longer than they thought to arrange its transport back here."

"Maybe. But I've got a bad feeling." Deborah's brow creased with worry.

In truth, Mary was dealing with her own worry. No matter how she looked at it, it was taking way too long for the men to return.

"I think we should pray," Mary said.

Deborah nodded, and both women bowed in silent prayer. They were interrupted by the crunch of gravel on the drive.

"They're here!" cried Mary, running to the door. She flung it open and Deborah crowded next to her. But it wasn't a horse and buggy. It was a car. Mary's heart froze when she saw the police emblem imprinted on its side.

Deborah grabbed her hand, squeezing it with a death clutch. Mary watched the car park and two officers get out and climb to the porch. They were both middle-aged men and somber-looking. The one who was quite pudgy, spoke.

"Is this the Zook residence?" he asked.

Deborah nodded.

"I'm sorry to inform you that there's been an accident…"

Mary's knees nearly buckled, and she would have fallen if not for Deborah's icy grip on her hand.

"Are they dead…?" Mary asked, her voice barely above a whisper.

"No, ma'am. They're both in the hospital here in Hollybrook. We can drive you there, if you wish."

Deborah looked at Mary, stark panic in her eyes. "I can't leave the *bopplis*…"

"I'll get my *mamm* to come and watch them." Mary gave a frantic look to the officer. "Can you drive me to my *mamm's* and then bring us back here?"

The officer looked at his partner then back to her. "Of course, ma'am."

"I need to notify Eli's kin. My parents…" Deborah muttered.

"My *dat* will do it. Don't worry."

Mary pried her hand loose from Deborah's and reached inside to grab her cape. "I'll be back soon," she told her friend. She followed the officers down the steps and climbed into the backseat of the car.

The officers were already buckled into the front. The heavy one, who was the driver, looked at her over the seat. "Where to?"

Mary gave him directions to her parents' farm. When the car pulled up to the porch, Mary jumped out and flew up the steps, bursting into the house. Her parents and brothers were around the table, eating.

"*Mamm*! Come quick! Deborah needs you. There's been an accident. Both our husbands are…" Mary gulped and forced herself to continue, "hurt and in the hospital. Come! Hurry!"

Everyone had risen from their seats.

"*Ach*! *Nee*!" cried her father.

"I'm coming," her mother said and rushed into the wash room for her coat.

"I'll follow in the buggy," her father said. "We'll meet you at the hospital."

"*Nee*," Mary pleaded. "I don't want you to drive at night. Please, *Dat*! Don't do it. Please just tell Deborah's and Eli's parents. Don't drive any farther than that. Come to the hospital in the morning."

Panic swirled through her.

"You don't worry about me, daughter. Just go. Go now."

Sandra had her coat on and the two of them rushed from the house. Mary almost stumbled down the steps, but she managed to stay upright. She climbed into the backseat with her mother. The officer pulled away immediately, heading back to Deborah's.

Deborah was pacing on the porch outside when they pulled up. Sandra grasped Mary's hand before she left the car. "It'll be all right," she said. "I'll be praying."

Then she was out of the car, climbing the steps to give Deborah a hug before disappearing inside. Deborah got into the car.

"I-I'm ready," she said to the officers.

Mary sat perched on the edge of the vinyl seat, the seatbelt straining across her chest. *Hurry*, she thought. *Hurry, hurry, hurry.* Her throat was dry, and her breathing turned shallow. She tried to swallow, but it was tight.

Be all right, she pleaded silently with Mark. *Be all right. We finally have a chance to start over. Please, please, dear Gott, let Mark be all right.*

Chapter Thirty-One

When they arrived at the hospital, the policeman from the passenger side escorted Mary and Deborah inside and deposited them in a nurse's care. They were immediately taken to a waiting room on the second floor.

"Wait here. A doctor will be with you shortly." The young woman regarded them both. "You'll have paperwork to fill out. I'll bring it to you."

Mary nodded, still trying to swallow past the dryness in her throat. Still trying to breathe. Deborah sank down onto a couch.

"Mary, he's going to die. I just know it. He's going to die."

Mary sat beside her and grabbed her hands. "*Nee*. He isn't. He *isn't*. He's going to be fine. You wait and see. He's going to be fine."

Deborah shook her head over and over. "I *knew* something was wrong. I knew it."

Within minutes, the nurse returned with two clipboards. "Here you are. I know you can't fill in everything that's on there. I've dealt with your kind before. Just fill out what you can."

Mary stared up at her. *Your kind?* Her mind was so befuddled that, at first, she didn't know what the nurse meant. Then, it came to her. Of course. The nurse had dealt with Amish folk before, which was no surprise since there was a fairly large district of them in Hollybrook. Mary took the clipboard from the woman and said nothing.

"I'll be back shortly to collect them. In the meantime, do your best."

Mary wanted to tell the woman that she was fully capable of reading and filling out a form. Who did the nurse think they were? Illiterate imbeciles? And then she recognized the futility of her anger. What difference did it make anyway?

But when she bent over the form, she realized that there were plenty of things she didn't know how to fill out properly. She had no insurance information. No family doctor. No history of disease. No phone numbers. She supposed she could give the number of the phone shanty down the road.

Deborah sat beside her, staring into space. Mary gently nudged her. "Deborah, you have to fill out the form."

Deborah turned her eyes to Mary. "A form? I couldn't care less about some stupid form! My husband is lying in here somewhere dying. My children won't have a father. I won't have anyone to help me…" Deborah crumpled against Mary's shoulder. "What am I going to do?"

Mary grew stern. "You're going to sit up and fill out that form. Then you're going to wait with me. That's what you're going to do."

Deborah lifted her head and gave Mary a scathing look. But then, she straightened and went to work on the form. Mary took a deep breath. How long before someone came and told them what was going on? She held the partially filled out form on her lap and stared at the large clock on the opposite wall. The second hand jerked its way through the minutes.

Deborah finished writing and dropped the clipboard onto the table that was filled with a jumble of magazines. "Where is the doctor?" she asked. She jumped up and began pacing. "Where is someone to help us?"

At that moment, the young nurse returned to collect the clipboards. She glanced over them and sighed.

"That's all we can tell you," Mary said, trying to manage her irritation.

"It'll have to do," the woman said and turned to go.

"Wait," Deborah cried. "What's happening? Why haven't we been told anything?"

The woman shrugged. "I'll see what I can find out, but the doctor will come out when he can."

Deborah lowered herself back to her chair. "What am I going to tell my *kinner*? They won't even remember Eli."

"Deborah, stop it! You don't know anything yet. Stop it." Mary's voice was firm.

Deborah sucked in a shaky breath. "*Nee*. You're right. You're right. *Gott* is here. He's here with us."

"*Jah*, he is. Concentrate on that."

"This place makes me nervous. This is the *Englisch* world. I don't like it."

"I don't either, but we've got no choice."

The elevator dinged, and Eli's parents came rushing into the room. "Deborah," they cried. "What happened?"

Deborah hurried over to them and explained as best she could. Then Deborah's parents showed up next.

Mary watched their stricken faces and watched Deborah try to keep her composure. She was glad that her own father hadn't shown up. He must have honored her wishes to wait until morning to come. Good. There was no reason for him to risk the drive in the dark. But no sooner had Mary thought so, when the elevator opened again, and Zeb came in. Despite herself, Mary breathed a sigh of relief to see him.

"Any news?" he asked, joining the group.

"Nothing yet," Mary said. She glanced toward the door at the back, assuming that was where the doctor would emerge.

They all sat down, except Eli's father. He paced a circle on the carpeted floor. Just when Mary was sinking in despair of ever hearing anything, the back door finally whooshed open and a doctor came out.

All of them turned.

He walked over, taking off his blue cap. "It was a bad accident," he said. "The driver of the car was killed."

"*Ach, nee,*" murmured Eli's mother.

"And Eli…" Deborah whispered. "Is he… Is he…"

The doctor looked at her. "Both Amish men are alive."

Mary's knees gave way, and her father caught her and pressed her against his side.

"Elijah Zook…? I'm sorry to inform you that his injuries were more severe. We had to… Well, we couldn't save his leg. We did everything we could."

A collective gasp went up. Deborah's face went completely white, and she grabbed her mother's arm.

"He will recover, and he'll need extensive therapy, but let's not worry about that now."

"Is he awake?" Eli's father choked out.

"No. But you can go in and see him. Two at a time please. The nurses will help you."

"And Mark Schrock?" Zeb asked, stepping closer to the doctor. "His injuries?"

"He's badly bruised. One rib is broken and his right leg is broken, but he should completely recover."

Mary breathed again, not even realizing that she'd been holding her breath.

"Can we see him?" Zeb asked.

"Come this way."

Mary looked at Deborah, who hadn't moved. Her expression was twisted, and she hardly looked like herself. Mary threw her arms around her. "It'll be all right," she whispered. "Somehow, it will be all right."

But Deborah remained stiff and unmoving in her arms.

"Come, Mary," her father said. "We need to see Mark."

Mary stumbled after him, going through the heavy door and entering a wide hallway.

"This way," the doctor said again and led them to a room.

Chapter Thirty-Two

Mary was afraid to go inside. When she screwed up her courage and entered the room, she saw Mark lying there, his leg suspended and a tube attached to his arm. His face was bruised and scratched, and his eyes were swollen and closed. He looked so helpless that Mary couldn't get a breath. She rushed forward and grasped his arm.

"Mark," she said softly. "*Ach*, Mark."

Zeb circled the bed. "When will he wake up?"

"It should be anytime," the doctor said. "If you need anything, press the call button." He started to leave the room and then seemed to think better of it. He walked back to the bed and picked up a white apparatus with buttons. "This is the call button. Just press it, and a nurse will come and help you."

Zeb nodded, and the doctor left.

Mary stood at Mark's side, silently weeping. He looked so vulnerable, so alone. She blinked away her tears, trying to better assess the damage.

"A broken rib, *Dat*? What do they do for that?"

"Just let it heal, as far as I know."

"Look at the cast on his leg. It's huge."

Zeb nodded. "We must thank *Gott* that he's alive. That he'll recover."

Mary began to sob. "Poor Deborah and Eli. What's going to happen? How can he farm with only one leg?"

Zeb shook his head. "Have you forgotten who you are, Mary? Have you forgotten where you come from?"

She wiped at her tears.

"Eli will have help. He will have the whole district to help him. You know that."

She did know that. She was ashamed of her tears. "I'm sorry."

Mark groaned, and Mary leaned over him. "Mark?"

His eyes fluttered open, and he groaned again.

"Mark, we're here now. You're all right."

He looked confused and blinked, looking around. His eyes found hers. "Eli? How's Eli?" His voice was scratchy and weak.

"He's here. In the hospital," Mary said. "He's alive. Deborah's with him."

Mark looked down at his leg that was suspended in air. His breath seeped out slowly. "What's wrong with me?"

Zeb stepped forward. "You've broken your leg and a rib. You're pretty banged up. Thank *Gott*, you're alive."

Mark nodded slowly.

"What happened?" Mary asked, brushing his hair from his forehead.

He closed his eyes. "We were…we were on our way back. Almost home. Some guy in a car ran us over on… on Elm Street. I think… Maybe, it was—"

"It's all right," Mary murmured, with her hand still on his hair. "I'm just so glad you're alive."

"Eli? He got it worse." Mark's voice hitched.

"He's all right," Mary said, her heart heavy.

"Mary?" Mark struggled to focus on her. "What is it?"

"You're tired," Zeb interrupted. "Sleep now."

Mark reached out and grabbed Mary's hand. "Tell me. What's wrong?"

Tears coursed down Mary's face. "*Dat's* right—"

"Mary." His voice was urgent, pleading.

Mary gave her father a desperate look and then turned to Mark. "Eli lost a leg. They couldn't save it."

Tears flooded Mark's eyes. "*Nee.*" He moaned. "*Nee.* Not his leg."

Zeb stepped forward. "He's alive. That's all that matters right now," he said. "We put our faith in *Gott.* You must rest, Mark. You need to rest."

Mark's eyes closed again, and Mary thought that maybe he'd drifted off. She tried to pry her hand from his grip, but he had a vice-like hold on her. She stretched behind herself and with her free hand, she pulled up a chair and sat down.

"I'll be staying here, *Dat.* Thank you for coming, but I'm sure *Mamm* is worried sick."

Zeb nodded. "The boys will want to know, too."

"They at home?"

"*Jah.* They wanted to come, but I made them stay put. They'll be here tomorrow."

"Thank you, *Dat.*"

He touched her shoulder. "I can take you home, if you want."

"*Nee.* I'm staying." She looked at her father and blinked back her tears. "You'll drive safely?"

"Of course, daughter. *Gott* is with me." He squeezed her shoulder and left the room.

She stared after him. *Gott is with me.* Then, why wasn't God with Eli and Mark when they were traveling? Why hadn't God saved them from this accident?

Guilt stung through her.

Who was she to question God?

The nurses came in regularly during the night to check on Mark. And Mark woke up more than a few times on his own. Each time, he would lurch and cry out Mary's name, only to fall back on the bed and groan. Mary did her best to comfort him. Once, during the wee hours of the morning, she tiptoed from the room to find Eli's room. He was on the same floor, but in a different section entirely. The night nurse wouldn't let her into the area, but Mary could see through the glass doors, and she saw Deborah and her mother sitting beside Eli's bed. Mary could barely make Eli out amidst all the machines and paraphernalia.

She stood by the nurse's desk and wept. Embarrassed at such a public display, she crept back down the hall to Mark's room.

By morning, Mary felt like her mouth was full of cotton. She was achy, tired, and hungry, but how could she complain? How could she even notice such things when Mark and Eli were hurting so? A different nurse came in and took Mark's vitals.

"Excuse me," Mary said.

The nurse, a plump middle-aged woman, turned to her with warm brown eyes. "Yes, honey?"

"My friend, Eli Zook, is also here. I was wondering if I could go see him?"

"Eli Zook? He was in the accident, too. I doubt they'll

let you in, but you're welcome to go check. Do you know where he is?"

Mary nodded. Mark grabbed her hand, and Mary jumped. "Mark? You're awake."

"You going to see Eli?"

"I'm going to try."

Mark's nostrils flared. The swelling around his eyes had gone down a bit, but he still looked almost ghoulish to her. "Tell him...tell him..." He couldn't continue.

Mary leaned close. "I will," she said. "I'll give him your love."

Mark squeezed his eyes shut, and Mary slipped out of the room.

Chapter Thirty-Three

Mary walked to the other end of the hallway. Before she reached the nurse's station, she saw Deborah, huddled against the wall.

"Deborah!" she uttered, going to her.

Deborah jerked around and looked at her. "How's Mark?"

"Recovering. And Eli?"

Deborah shook her head and clutched Mary's arm. "What are we going to do? Eli and me? What's going to happen to us?"

"Nothing's going to happen to you. You're going to be fine," Mary said, trying to muster every bit of confidence into her voice. "We're all here to help you. You know that."

"Eli isn't…" Deborah covered her mouth.

"He's going to be fine."

"He isn't… He doesn't talk. He won't look at me."

Mary's throat tightened. "Give him time. He's not himself. I'm sure the *Englisch* doctors have put him on all sorts of drugs."

"His leg is gone, Mary," Deborah said, her voice thick

with tears. "Did they throw it away? Where is it? Is it in some garbage can somewhere?"

Mary blinked. She had no idea, nor did she know what to say. She took Deborah's arm and led her to a bench. "It's going to be fine," she mumbled, feeling how empty her words were.

"Rachel will be hungry," Deborah said. "I'm not there to nurse her. *Mamm* went to fetch her. She wanted me to go home, but I wouldn't go. She's going to bring the *boppli* to me."

Mary had no idea whether babies were allowed in hospital rooms or not, but she didn't say anything.

"And little Ross is probably scared, wondering where his *mamm* and *dat* are."

"He's with his *grossmammi* now. He'll be all right and so will Rachel. Will Rachel take a bottle?"

Deborah frowned. "My *bopplis* don't take bottles, Mary." Her voice was tense and then her expression crumpled. "I'm sorry."

"No need." Mary rubbed Deborah's back. "It's going to be all right."

How many times would she have to say that before even she believed it? She harbored the same doubts, the same confusion that Deborah did, but she couldn't admit it. She needed to be strong for her friend. For Eli. For Mark.

"I'm so tired," Deborah said, slumping against Mary. "I didn't know a body could be this tired."

"Maybe, you can rest a bit today," Mary murmured.

"I can't leave Eli. I can't."

"I know."

The two friends sat together, neither moving, for a

long time. Eli's mother came out to the hallway and saw them.

"Deborah? He's awake again."

Deborah shot up and rushed off. Mary watched her go, her heart aching with every step Deborah took. Nancy Zook sat down beside her. She sighed heavily. "How is your man?" she asked.

"He's doing all right," Mary said.

"So, he broke his rib and his leg. And he's in traction or something?"

Mary nodded.

"It's all such a tragedy," Nancy whispered, her hand over her mouth. "Such a tragedy."

"I'm so sorry," Mary said. "About Eli. Deeply sorry."

Nancy straightened her back and took a deep breath. "*Gott* is *gut*. We will trust him."

"*Jah. Gott* is *gut*." Mary regarded the woman, admiring her courage. Because right then, Mary was mortified to realize that she wasn't thinking about God's goodness at all. She was thinking about her lost baby and Eli's lost leg. If God was so good…

But no. She knew better than to let her mind wander there.

"I need to get back to Mark," Mary said, standing.

"You get back to your husband," Nancy said. "I need to get back to Eli, too."

Mary walked partway down the hall and then looked back over her shoulder. Nancy hadn't moved. She was sitting very still, staring into space, her face frozen in an expression of grief.

At mid-morning, Sandra Hochstetler burst into Mark's room. "Where's my son-in-law?" she asked.

Upon seeing Mark, she hurried to his bedside and grabbed his hand.

"Hello," Mark said.

Sandra looked at his leg and all the humming machines. "Lands' sake. Look at all this. How are you, son?"

"Coping," he said. He glanced at Mary, and she gave him an encouraging smile.

"Of course, you are." Sandra looked at Mary. "You're tired. Your *dat* is seeing Eli right now. Afterward, he can take you home for some rest."

"I'm not leaving, *Mamm*."

Mark gazed at her. "Go on home, Mary. You need to sleep. I know you were up all night."

"*Nee*. I'm fine. I'm not leaving."

A nurse came into the room. "The doctor will be in shortly," she said. "We'll be removing the traction."

"I thought he'd need it longer," Mary said.

"Used to be that way. Not anymore. Last night, it was used because of the trauma and to help with pain relief. It's not necessary anymore." She fiddled with some of the instruments and then looked at Mark. "What's your pain level?"

Mark glanced at Mary before responding. "A five."

"Five?" the nurse repeated, alarmed. "That's much too high. I'll adjust your meds."

When the nurse left, Sandra went to Mary and gazed at her. "You'll need to go home eventually, Mary. I can sit with Mark today. It will give you a chance for a rest and a bath."

"*Mamm*," Mary said, working to keep her voice even. "I'm not leaving."

Sandra shrugged. "All right, dear. I'm going to go see Nancy Zook." She squeezed Mark's arm and left.

An uneasy silence filled the room. Mary shifted in her seat. Mark closed his eyes, and she hoped he would sleep some more.

"I talked to Isaac," he said, opening his eyes and staring at her.

She sucked in her breath. "What?"

"You heard me."

She stood and inched closer to his bed. "When? What do you mean?"

"After you left for Linnow Creek. After the... miscarriage." He licked his lips.

"Why? What did you say?" Mary's insides went cold.

"I told him to leave."

"Leave?"

"I told him to leave Hollybrook and never come back."

Mary stepped back. "You did?" She could hardly believe what she was hearing.

"I did." His voice was clipped and surprisingly strong for someone lying in a hospital bed as injured as he was.

"What did he say?"

"Does it matter?"

It didn't. Not really. But Mary wanted to know. It had been about her, after all. "I suppose it doesn't."

His eyes were intent on hers. "But you want to know anyway."

She felt like she was balancing on the edge of a cliff. If she said the wrong thing, she would fall headlong into an abyss and never climb out.

"*Nee.* I don't want to know." She swallowed and arranged her features in what she hoped was a neutral expression.

"He was angry," Mark said. "He told me it wasn't my business."

"So, you knew he'd come to see me in Linnow Creek before I told you?"

"*Nee*. I didn't know."

Mary wondered whether Isaac had come to see her after Mark had talked to him or before. But Isaac had shown up in Linnow Creek right away. Her guess was that he'd come before Mark spoke to him.

"Are you angry?" Mark asked.

"*Nee*," she said quickly. "*Nee*."

But she did have to digest the news. She wondered whether Isaac had heeded Mark's edict and left Hollybrook. Deborah had told her that Isaac hadn't been to church service lately. Was he already gone? She backed away and sank down into her chair. Well, it didn't matter to her. She didn't even want to think about it.

Her overriding task now was to help Mark get better. To get him back home. To take care of him.

Mark was watching her and then his eyes fell shut as if he couldn't hold them open any longer. He looked completely drained. She waited a moment and then got up and tiptoed to his side, leaning over until her face was close to his. His breathing was soft and regular, and she felt an odd sense of comfort as his breath brushed over her skin. She kissed his lips softly and was about to stand up, when he reached out and grabbed her arm, pulling her close.

He kissed her then, his mouth covering hers. There was a desperation to the kiss that stunned her. But she tried to relax into him, kissing him back. When they broke apart, his eyes searched hers. Finally, she smiled and backed away.

"Sleep now," she whispered and left the room.

Chapter Thirty-Four

Outside, in the hallway, Mary slumped against the closed door and caught her breath. Mark needed to come home. She *wanted* him home. She wanted out of this hospital. Wanted out of this *Englisch* world. She wanted Mark to be all right—wanted Eli to be all right.

"Maria?"

Mary's heart lurched, and she turned her head. She gaped at Isaac. "What are *you* doing here?" Dread and fear and anger all rose up, fighting within her. "You can't be here. Why did you come?"

She clasped the door handle behind her back. Would Isaac *never* leave her alone? *Never* go away?

Isaac shook his head and held up both hands. "I'm not here for you. Maria. *I'm not here for you.*"

She sucked in air and gazed at him suspiciously. "Then what *are* you doing here?"

"We've all heard about the accident. I'm here to see Eli. Maybe you've forgotten that Eli and I used to be *gut* friends. Then I'm gone."

She shrank back against the wood of the door, folding into herself. She prayed no one would see her talking to

Isaac. She prayed their voices wouldn't pass through the door and reach Mark's ears.

"I'm sorry about your husband, too." Isaac paused within a couple feet from her. "I—well, I'm sorry."

She didn't respond, but her eyes didn't leave his.

"I'll go see Eli now," he said, but his feet didn't move.

"You can't be here," she whispered. "You *can't…*"

"I'm leaving Hollybrook. I'm going back to the *Englisch* world. I don't belong here, Maria. As you've so plainly said."

Her throat went dry, and she tried to swallow. Her eyes were wide and unblinking on him.

"So, you see. You can rejoice now. You'll never have to see me again." His hands dropped to his sides, and the look on his face was pained.

It was then that she noticed he was wearing *Englisch* shoes. They were white with rubber soles and long shoelaces, even though the rest of his attire was Amish. He looked strange, a person trapped between two worlds.

He noticed her attention on his sneakers. He picked up a foot and gave a rueful chuckle. "Jogging shoes," he told her. "They're really comfortable."

She stared at him.

"Good-bye, Maria."

She opened her mouth to respond, but her voice wouldn't come. He left her with a sidelong glance from the corner of his hazel eyes. She nodded ever so slightly, almost as if she hadn't made any gesture at all. But he must have noticed because he nodded back. Then he gave her a jaunty two-finger salute and turned away.

She watched him walk down the hall. So, this was it. *For sure and for certain, this time.* She was never to see Isaac again. He would likely return to Indianapolis, a place where she never went. There was no cause. Everything she could possibly want or need was right there in Hollybrook.

Three days later, Mark was released from the hospital. The doctor informed them that he would need extensive physical therapy once his cast was removed. Mary only listened with half an ear. She would deal with all of that later. Right then, the only thing she cared about was that Mark was coming home.

Her father transported them in his wagon. Zeb was concerned that the closed buggy would prove problematic with Mark's large cast. Mary layered Mark with quilts in the bed of the wagon and sat on the front bench with her father. The air was bitterly cold, but she huddled inside her coat and scarf and sat stoically until they pulled up to her front porch.

She jumped down and ran around to the back of the wagon. By the white, pinched look on Mark's face, Mary knew he was miserable and in no small amount of pain.

Zeb circled the wagon to help her get Mark down. Mark shrugged off Mary's help and leaned heavily on Zeb. Mary tried not to let his rebuff bother her—soon enough, he'd have no choice but to lean on her.

"I'll go inside to get the fire going," she told her father. "I thought we could set him up in the front room."

"Don't talk about me like I'm not here," Mark said. "And I can maneuver myself just fine with the crutches."

Perhaps that was true, but Mary knew the ordeal was taking a large toll on him.

"I'm here, and I'm helping you," Zeb said resolutely, heaving Mark fully down from the back of the wagon.

Mark groaned and quickly put his crutches under his arms.

Mary turned away and hurried inside. She stirred up the banked fire, and it came to life. She stuck in a good-sized log and closed the heavy doors. Mark made his way into the front room and collapsed on the davenport.

"Thank you, *Dat*," Mary said. She went to Mark and tried to drape an afghan over him, but he resisted.

"I'm not cold."

Mary turned to her father. "Will you stay for a meal?"

"*Nee*, daughter. I'll be heading home. I'll send Jerrod over early tomorrow to help with the outside chores. Your brother will be glad to come."

"That isn't necessary," Mary protested. "I can do the chores. It's winter, and there isn't that much to be done."

"That cow ain't gonna milk herself, and you'll have plenty to do in the house," Zeb said. "Plus, the other animals have to be tended, and there's always chores to be done outside. Even in the cold. I'm sending Jerrod over."

"All right," Mary said, giving in. "I'll look for him."

Zeb left, and Mary turned to her husband. He was leaning back against the cushion, and his expression was haggard.

"I'm going to make tea."

Mark winced and gazed at her. "I'm not wanting any tea. I need to get out to the barn and look after the animals. I'm going to rest for a few minutes is all. And you were right. I don't need Jerrod's help."

"You're not going out to the barn," she protested. "You're in no condition to do anything right now. You just ask, and I'll see to it that whatever it is, gets done."

Mark looked annoyed, but he didn't say anything. But Mary knew her husband; this discussion wasn't over.

"Eli's going to be in the hospital for up to two weeks," she said. "I'll need to go to Deborah's now and again, to see to things."

"His family will do it."

She stopped and looked at him. He was staring down at the large white cast on his leg. She wondered whether he'd actually taken the painkillers the nurse had handed him before they left his room. He looked rough and so uncomfortable that Mary's heart squeezed with sympathy.

"Mark? Did you take the pills?"

He raised his eyes to hers. "I don't favor *Englisch* medicine."

She sighed. "I know you don't, but it's only for a while longer."

"I'll need to go back there again and again for therapy. You heard the doctor."

"I did. It's a small price to pay for the full use of your leg again."

"I want to see Old Mae."

"Of course," she said, more than willing to fetch the district's medicine woman. "I'll go get her real soon."

"Thank you." He grunted.

Mary sat down next to him, which was awkward as his leg was stretched diagonally across the davenport. But she squeezed in beside him anyway, yearning to be close to him.

"Mark?" she said softly.

He looked at her.

"I'm so thankful you're all right." Her voice broke, and she fought against sudden tears.

For the slightest moment, he looked doubtful, and then his expression cleared. "*Gott* is *gut*," he said.

She reached out and took his hand. "I don't know what I would have done if you'd been killed."

He inhaled slowly. "I reckon you'd have found yourself some other man."

She went stiff. His words hovered over them, and she pulled her hand back. "How can you say that?"

His face flushed red. "I'm sorry," he muttered. "I'm sorry."

"That was truly unkind." She wriggled out from behind his leg and stood.

He grabbed her hand. "You're right. I don't know what I was thinking. I'm sorry."

She looked down at his strong fingers gripping hers. "You're not yourself, right now," she said softly. "It's all right."

She tugged free of his hand and went to the kitchen. Methodically, she filled the kettle and set it on the cook stove. She got out two cups and two teabags. She set the jar of honey next to the cups. Then she leaned against the counter and waited for the water to get hot.

Chapter Thirty-Five

Mary set up a bed for Mark on the davenport. It was simply too hard for him to maneuver the steps at that point. When she awoke early the next morning, she quickly got dressed and hurried downstairs.

Mark was awake, sitting in the near dark, watching the doorway.

"*Gut* morning," she said.

"Morning."

"Did you sleep well?"

"Mary? Can you come in here, please?"

"Of course." She hurried into the room and stood beside his makeshift bed.

"I'm right sorry about last night. I don't have much of an excuse. I was hurting, but that didn't give me leave to be cruel."

Mary's throat tightened. "It's all right, Mark. I know you weren't yourself."

"Still…"

She patted his shoulder. "It's all right. I'm going out to see to the animals. Do you want something to eat first?"

"*Nee*."

It was too dark to make out his features well. She leaned down and kissed his cheek. "I'll be back quick-like."

"Don't hurry for me," he said. "I'm not going anywhere."

She went to put on her heavy shoes and coat and scarf. She peered through the window. A bit of light showed in the east, but not enough to see much of anything. She felt for the lantern on the shelf by the side door and lit it. Bracing herself, she opened the door and stepped outside. There was a hollow silence in the frigid air. She shivered and started across the yard.

She held the lantern out in front of her and headed for the barn. She heard the goats before she even got to the door. She chuckled and pulled open the heavy door.

"I'm here," she called out cheerily.

Their cow gave a low bellow. Before she could even hang the lantern on the protruding nail, two of the goats were by her side. Millie, their Alpine, leapt up, putting her two front hooves on Mary's waist.

"Millie! You little stinker, you! Get on down, so I can get your feed."

But Millie only butted her nose against Mary's chest. And then Oscar, one of their male goats, joined Millie, nearly knocking Mary off her feet.

"You silly things! Get down, now." Mary laughed and grabbed their hooves, placing them back on the ground, which only served to start a game. The goats jumped up on her again and again as she tried to move across the barn. She nearly tripped on a hoe than had slipped away from the bales of hay where it had been resting.

"Whoa!" Mary cried, righting herself.

"Mary?"

Mary turned to see her brother's silhouette framing the doorway. "Jerrod. You're here."

Jerrod laughed. "In the nick of time, it seems." He walked to her and pushed the goats aside. "Didn't *Dat* tell you I was coming?"

"He did."

"Then why are you out here? I'll see to the animals. Although, milking goats ain't exactly my favorite thing to do."

Mary shrugged. "You and I both know that goat's milk makes the best cheese."

"That it does. But give me a cow to milk any old day."

Mary laughed. "We've got one of those, too."

"I know you do. Listen, go on back into the house. I'll finish up here."

Mary wiped her hands down her coat. "All right. Thanks, Jerrod."

"Can I come in to see Mark when I'm done?"

"Of course, you can. I'll make enough breakfast for you." Mary lit one of the lanterns they kept out in the barn and then took hers off the nail. "Mark will be right glad to see you."

Jerrod nodded. "Me, too."

Mary left the barn and hurried across the yard to the house. "Jerrod's here," she called out, as she stepped inside.

"Is he?" Mark replied.

She heard some rustling and then a steady thumping as Mark crossed the floor.

"No need to get up," she told him. "I'll get breakfast on."

"I need to go out and help Jerrod."

Mary grimaced. "You don't need to do any such

thing. He's perfectly capable of seeing to the animals. He'll be in for breakfast when he's finished."

She set the lantern down on the dining table, and then she turned to Mark. She went to him and slipped her arms around his waist. He wavered slightly, and she tightened her grip.

"Sorry," she mumbled. "I don't want to knock you over."

He didn't return her embrace as both his hands and arms were busy with the crutches, but he leaned down and kissed the top of her *kapp*.

"I don't want to be a burden," he said.

She backed up and gazed into his eyes. "A burden?" She shook her head. "You're no burden." Her voice broke, and she cleared her throat. "*I've* been the burden." She shuddered. "But that's all in the past now. From this point on, neither of us will be a burden. How about that?"

She smiled bravely, praying Mark would smile in return. When he did, her spirits soared.

"Are we starting over?" he asked.

"We are." She nodded and turned to pick up the lantern. "I'm going into the kitchen now. Would you kindly go sit back down? I'll call you when the food is ready."

He shook his head, and her smile faded.

"I'm not sitting back down, Mary. I have to use the bathroom." His voice was light.

Mary laughed. Was he teasing her? Being playful? A lump formed in her throat, and she went to him. "How about I help you up the stairs then?"

"How about I step outside? No stairs. Well, just the two or three." He gave her a mischievous grin.

"Mark Schrock, you are scandalous!"

His eyes widened. "Am I?"

She stepped back. "Outside it is, then." She walked slightly ahead of him and opened the side door. "Go on with you? Don't you want a coat?"

"It isn't going to take me more than a few seconds to do my business," he said, and she could still hear the light-heartedness in his voice.

Chapter Thirty-Six

❧

Their days fell into a rhythm. Jerrod came by every morning to care for the animals and to do whatever other outside chores were necessary. Mary always fixed enough breakfast for him, and he joined them around the table every morning when he was finished. He and Mark kept the conversation lively, talking about crops and animals and any new-fangled machinery that Jerrod had heard about. Mary listened in, feeling content and comfortable with how things were going.

Mark seemed more approachable every day. Sometimes, he even pulled her down for a kiss. When she responded warmly, though, he'd stiffen and release her, as if wary of getting too close. As if wary of trusting her.

On the sixth morning after Mark came home from the hospital, Mary went to him after breakfast.

"I think I need to check on Deborah," she told him. "Eli's still in the hospital, and Deborah has been going back and forth. I thought to take a casserole over to her place and see if she needs anything else."

Mark nodded. "*Jah.* I think you should, but I can't drive you over."

"I know. I'll take the pony cart."

"It's bitter cold out there."

"I know, but I've already got some bricks warming on the stove. And you know Flame. He'll be glad for the outing."

Mark chuckled. "That he will."

"Do you need anything before I go?"

He shook his head. "Be careful, Mary. There could be ice."

"I will. I'll go real slow. The casserole is ready, so I'm going to head out now." She leaned forward and kissed his cheek. "Bye."

"Bye," he murmured.

She went into the wash room and bundled up. Then she returned to the kitchen and covered the casserole in aluminum foil and then folded a towel around it. She carried it outside and set it in the pony cart. Her hands already felt half-frozen, but she had never gotten the knack of hitching Flame up with her mittens on, so she wouldn't bother to put them on until the horse was ready.

She took Flame from his stall and brought him outside to the cart. Her teeth were chattering by the time she got him hitched.

"The bricks!" she cried, having totally forgotten about them. She ran back to the house and rushed inside. Using hot pads, she wrapped the hot bricks in the old rags she kept under the sink just for that purpose.

"Mary? That you?" Mark called from the front room.

"*Jah!* I forgot the bricks. I'm taking them out now."

"All right."

She hugged the bricks close and ran back outside to the cart. Flame stomped twice and blew out his breath in a cloud of white.

"I'm back," she told him. "Don't get so impatient."

She climbed onto the driver's bench and positioned the bricks at her feet. She saved one to put in her lap. Most folks didn't do that, but she loved the feeling of the heat once it sank through the layers of her cape and dress. She picked up the reins and flicked them on Flame's backside. The cart jolted as Flame broke into an immediate trot. Mary laughed. The poor horse was itching to hurry down the road. She kept her grip taut, however, not wanting to risk sliding over the icy asphalt.

Once Flame had pulled the cart into the well-worn grooves at the side of the road, Mary relaxed a bit, her thoughts going to Deborah. Mary hoped she would catch her at home. She supposed she could go into town to the hospital if necessary, but that would take a lot more time, and she didn't want Mark to worry.

There was no one on the road, and she made good time. She pulled up to Deborah's house and saw movement through the window. She secured Flame and went inside without bothering to knock.

"Deborah?" she ventured.

Deborah emerged from the kitchen with Rachel in her arms. "*Ach!* Mary. It's you."

Mary went to her, shedding her cape and draping it over a bench at the table. "*Jah*. It's me." She reached out for Rachel and took the child, snuggling her against her chest.

Deborah's shoulders slumped. "You're a welcome sight," she said. "Would you like some tea?"

"Why don't you sit down and let me make it?" Mary suggested. "Where's Ross?"

Deborah looked around. "He's somewhere playing, I imagine. And *jah*, I'll take you up on that tea."

Mary went into the kitchen and fussed about, knowing her way around. It was a bit more difficult with the baby on her hip, but she didn't mind. The good Lord willing, she'd soon have her own babe to balance on her hip. The water in the kettle was already warm, so Mary had the tea ready quickly. She carried the first cup out to the table.

"I put a touch of honey in it. Just like you prefer."

Deborah took the cup in her hands and breathed in the steam rising from the cup. "Thank you, Mary."

Mary went to fetch her cup and then joined Deborah at the table. "How is Eli?"

Deborah blinked back sudden tears. "He's improving. The doctors say he can come home later this week."

"Is he still in pain?"

"They've got him all drugged up with those *Englisch* drugs. Old Mae's been to see him."

"What does she say?"

"She brought her herbs and such. She told me that she'll be coming over as soon as he's home."

"And his...well, his leg?" Mary frowned. "I mean, well..."

"I know what you mean. He's healing." Deborah took a sip of tea. "They're going to fit him with a temporary false leg before he leaves the hospital if it heals enough and if the swelling goes down. The doctor says he can get a permanent leg in two to three months, depending on how his...his stump heals."

Mary nodded. "How does he feel about that?"

Deborah set her cup down and took a deep breath. "He won't talk to me about it. He won't talk to anyone about it. I don't even know if he'll use a false leg."

"Surely, he will," Mary interrupted. "It would make a huge difference."

"Do you have any idea how much this is going to cost? Between five and *fifty* thousand dollars."

Mary gasped. She'd had no idea.

"And he'll need a new one every five years or so." Deborah closed her eyes and let out her breath. "Costs like that will wipe out the district's funds."

"But that's why we have them," Mary said, still trying to wrap her mind around such an exorbitant amount.

"Eli won't be liking the fact that it's on account of him that the district will lose most of its resources."

"But people will give more to the emergency fund. You know that."

"Eli won't like it."

"But he would do the same for someone else in the district."

Deborah looked at her, the shadows under her eyes pronounced. "I know that. But I also know my husband. He isn't going to like it. That's why I'm afraid he'll say no. And that cost is in addition to the hospital costs, mind you."

Mary nodded. "I know. We haven't seen any bills from Mark's stay yet. And he's not done, either. He has to have physical therapy."

"How's he doing?"

"Tolerable well."

"And the two of you?"

It wasn't common to ask such personal questions, but Mary didn't mind Deborah asking. The two of them had been friends for so long, and they'd been brutally honest with each other many times in the past.

"I think we're better. Not where I want to be, but better."

Deborah reached over and squeezed Mary's hand.

"Mark told Isaac to leave town," Mary blurted.

Deborah sucked in her breath. "Did he?"

Mary nodded.

"But I saw Isaac at the hospital. He came in to see Eli, so he isn't gone."

"I know. But I'm sure he is by now. He's going back to the *Englisch*. Back to Indianapolis."

Deborah put her hand over her mouth. "It's a *gut* thing, then," she murmured. "A *gut* thing that you two didn't work out."

Mary shifted Rachel on her lap. "I can't help but think he would have stayed if we'd have been together."

Deborah shook her head. "*Nee. Nee.* He had that streak in him. He would have broken your heart even more."

Mary rubbed her forehead and then bounced Rachel on her knee. "Let's not talk about him anymore. Are you going in to the hospital today?"

Deborah's brow raised, but she went with the change of subject. "I go in every day. I take the children to Eli's *mamm*, and she watches them till I come home."

Mary glanced around the house. "And what needs to be done around here?"

"Eli's *dat* takes care of the animals. I've been able to keep up with the rest. I'm only here part of the day, so it doesn't get messy. And I don't have to cook anything but the morning meal. I eat with Eli's family when I go to fetch the *kinner*."

Mary looked at her friend. "And you? How are *you* doing?"

"I'm fine," Deborah answered quickly. Too quickly.

"Deborah. You know all my terrible secrets, so I'm going to ask you again. How are you doing?"

Deborah's face crumpled. "I'm trying. Really, I am. But I'm exhausted, and I'm afraid." She looked at Mary with tears in her eyes. "I'm *afraid*, Mary, and I'm supposedly a woman of faith."

Mary grabbed her arm. "You *are* a woman of faith."

Rachel began to fuss so Mary stood up and bounced the baby gently back and forth, shifting her weight from one foot to the other. "In time, your fear will lessen. There's just so many unknowns."

"If I really had faith, I wouldn't be afraid."

Mary's heart went out to her friend. "Don't do that—"

"Do what?"

"Put more pressure on yourself than you already have. You can be afraid if you need to be. *Gott* is with you, and he understands. Your fear will fade in time."

"*Gott* can't be too pleased with my fear, and I can't pretend that he is."

Mary breathed out softly. "Sometimes, I think we put too much pressure on ourselves. Sometimes, I think we make *Gott* out to be much more judgmental than he really is."

"Mary!" Deborah cried, aghast. "You can't be saying such things. What if Bishop heard you?"

"Then he'd know that I've been thinking about *Gott*. He'd know that I've been pondering spiritual things."

"He'd know that you're bordering on rebellious, is what he'd know."

Mary sighed. "I suppose you're right. But I still wonder…"

"It isn't your job to wonder, Mary. It's your job to follow the *Ordnung*."

Mary bristled. "I follow the rules."

Deborah stood and picked up both their cups. "Of course, you do. I'm sorry. Don't mind me. I'm not myself these days."

Mary followed her to the kitchen counter. She noted the stack of dirty dishes in the sink. It was so surprising and unexpected that she worked to control her facial expression. Deborah's kitchen was always spotless.

Deborah balanced the two dirty cups on top of the array of dishes. "I should get to these," she said vaguely.

"*Nee*. You do what you need to do to get ready to go to the hospital. I can whip up these dishes in no time."

Deborah's eyes misted over. "Would you?"

"Of course. Go get ready."

Deborah took Rachel from Mary's arms and left the kitchen. Mary went to the sink and took out the dirty dishes one by one, setting them on the counter. Then she filled the sink with hot water and began washing the dishes, placing them in the drainer to dry.

Fifty thousand dollars? Mary could hardly comprehend such an amount. But Eli needed to walk. Otherwise, there was no way he could work the farm. And if he couldn't work the farm, her friend's family was going to be destitute mighty fast. Either that, or they would become a continual drain on the community. Something Eli would hate and never allow.

No. He needed that false leg.

She scrubbed the cast iron skillet with extra vigor, trying to imagine if she were in Deborah's position…

if it had been Mark who had lost his leg. She couldn't fathom it.

She just couldn't.

Chapter Thirty-Seven

On her way back to the farm, Mary decided to drive by Old Mae's and see if the woman was home. She was eager to have her see Mark. Eager to get her opinion on how he was healing. When she pulled the cart into Mae's property, she spotted the elderly woman out by the side of her house. She was beating on a braided rug which she'd hung from her clothesline.

Mary stopped the cart, secured Flame, and ran to help Old Mae. She took the broom from her hands and started beating the rug herself.

Old Mae chuckled. "I'm fully capable of pounding my own rugs, Mary Schrock."

"I know that," Mary said. "But how many hundreds of times have you helped us?"

The woman shrugged.

"There doesn't seem to be much more dirt flying out of this," Mary observed. "I think I'm a bit late to be helping."

Old Mae took the broom back. "You can help by taking the rug down and bringing it back into the house."

Mary unpinned the rug from the line, shocked at how

heavy the thing was. She sagged under its weight as she wrestled it back into the house.

"Right in here." Old Mae directed her into the front room.

Mary dropped the rug in the middle of the room and then busied herself straightening it out and putting the edges under the davenport. She stood back and looked at it. "Fresh as a daisy," she said and laughed.

"I know it ain't the time to be beating rugs outside, but this one looked so tired and droopy that I couldn't help myself."

"In truth, I don't know how you got it out there and on the line. It must weigh a hundred pounds."

"*Nee.* Not a hundred, though it does feel like it." Old Mae sat in one of her rockers. "What can I do for you?"

Mary sat down on the davenport. "I wondered if I might take you to my place so you can see Mark. Check on him. I'll drive you back home afterward."

"I can hitch up my own cart and drive myself."

"I know, but let me take you. I'm already here. My cart is already hitched. And you know Flame. Any excuse for additional outings is fine with him." Mary didn't want Old Mae hitching up her own cart. It was cold and slippery out. Mary was happy to transport her.

Old Mae stood. "All right. And I'm eager to see Mark. I went in to the hospital a couple days ago and saw Eli." She shook her head. "A crying shame, that one. Losing his leg like that."

"I feel so badly about it."

"So do we all. But he'll be getting his false leg soon enough."

"If he'll accept it."

"He'll accept it," Old Mae stated and left the room.

Mary watched her go. How did Mae know Eli would accept it? Yet, the medicine woman seemed to know many things before they happened. When Mary was young, she thought Old Mae had magical powers. And maybe, she did. In any case, if Old Mae said Eli would accept the leg, then Eli would accept the leg.

Old Mae returned, all bundled up in her black cape, bonnet, and mittens. They both went outside and got into the cart. The ride was cold, the still air hovering like an encasement surrounding them. Mary didn't need to do much to guide Flame. Old Mae sat perfectly still beside Mary. More than once, Mary glanced at her to make sure she was all right, which she always was.

Mary pulled into her long driveway and the gravel crunched and crackled beneath them. She drove straight up to the porch to let Old Mae out.

"Go on in," Mary said. "I'll see to Flame and be in shortly."

"No need to unhitch him," Mae told her. "I won't stay long."

"You're welcome to join us for supper."

The woman shook her head and looked up to study the sky. "Going to be a storm later. I'll need to be at home."

Mary followed her gaze upward. It looked perfectly ordinary with a thick layer of low white clouds blanketing the sky. A storm didn't look imminent at all.

"All right," Mary said, not wanting to argue with the wise woman. "I'll just come in with you then."

She clambered out of the cart and climbed the steps. She held the front door open for Old Mae, and they both went inside. The warmth curled around Mary, and she smiled. It was always good to come in out of the cold.

"Mark?" she called. "Old Mae is here."

She looked at Old Mae. "He's in the front room. Go ahead in. I'll make us all some tea."

Old Mae disappeared into the front room, and Mary hustled to the kitchen. She had the kettle on within minutes and the teacups out, each with a dollop of honey in the bottom and a teabag on the side. She waited for the water to heat up, wanting to give Mark and Old Mae some privacy. In truth, she was dying to hear what the woman had to say, but she sensed that Mark wouldn't want her in there.

When the kettle began to whistle, she finished preparing the tea. She filled the tray, adding a small plate with slices of bread on it. She carried it into the front room and set it on the coffee table.

Old Mae was sitting next to Mark, holding his hand in hers.

Mark looked up. "Mary."

"Hello, Mark," she said quietly. "I've brought some tea and bread."

Old Mae reached for a cup and blew on it a bit before taking a sip. "Ahh. This honey is right *gut*. Did you get it from Rhoda's bees?"

Mary nodded. "I did."

Old Mae took another sip. "Delicious." She took a folded white cloth from her waistband. "Here," she said to Mary. "I've already told Mark that I want him to drink this morning and night for at least the next week. It'll soothe his pain and speed the healing."

Mary unfolded the square of cloth and saw that it was full of dried herbs. "All right. I'll see to it."

Old Mae set her cup back on the tray. "I need to get back home before the storm sets in. Mary, you won't want to be out in it, either."

Mary stood. "I'm ready to take you."

Mark scowled. "A storm's coming?"

"*Jah*. But Mary will make it back in time. Don't you worry."

"You can stay the night, Mae," he said. "I don't want anyone caught in a storm."

Old Mae clucked her tongue. "Now. Now. I won't be sleeping anywhere but my own bed. Good-bye, Mark. I'll check with you in a week or so."

Mark's scowl didn't fade. "Mary…"

"Don't fret," Mary said. "I'll just take her home and come right back." She felt an urge to kiss him on the cheek before she left, but she decided against it. He still seemed hesitant about her physical affection, and they weren't alone anyway. She didn't know if she could stand Old Mae watching Mark tense up when she went to kiss him good-bye.

She hurried to the pegs by the front door where she'd hung both their capes. She handed Old Mae hers and after bundling up, they both went outside. The temperature had dropped significantly. Mary shivered and looked up at the sky. No change in the cloud formations. She wondered again if Old Mae was right about the storm.

Flame broke into a steady trot, and the cart fell into a nice rhythm as they headed toward Old Mae's farm. When Mary guided Flame into Mae's drive, the woman put her hand on Mary's arm.

"Patience," she said. "That's what he needs. Patience. And all the help and love you can give him."

Mary's eyes filled with tears. She nodded and tugged on the reins. Old Mae looked at her with her sharp grey eyes.

"You're doing a right *gut* job, Mary. I'm glad you're back. Glad you left Linnow Creek and came back to us. Mark's glad, too."

"Is he?" Mary asked.

"*Jah*. Don't doubt that, girl. Things will be different a year from now. You'll be cradling your own *boppli*, and life will be sweet."

Mary's heart fluttered. "Will I, Mae? Will I have my own *boppli*?"

Old Mae leaned close, her wizened face breaking into a wide smile. "Don't you remember what I told you, child? After you lost your wee one? I said there will be others. Many, many others."

"I remember." Mary's voice was quiet.

"Hang onto that. Hang onto *Gott*." Old Mae released her arm and lumbered out of the cart. At the top of her porch steps, she turned and waved at Mary.

Chapter Thirty-Eight

Mary waved back at Old Mae and then snapped the reins, heading for home. She hadn't gone more than a mile when the sky darkened and the first splats of slushy rain mixed with ice dropped on her nose. She glanced up, squinting, as the drops came faster. A wind came up, blowing her scarf up into her face. She snatched it down and bent her head into the squall.

Old Mae had been right. A storm was definitely brewing. Mary loosened the reins and whipped them over Flame's back. "Come on, boy. Let's speed up now. Come on."

Flame sensed her urgency and increased his speed. The wind was blowing hard, slapping against Mary's face. She lowered her head and braced herself against the onslaught. The rain turned harder, icier, and she dreaded what it was doing to the road. Thankfully, she didn't have much farther to go.

"Come on, Flame! Let's get home," she hollered.

A car zoomed by, causing the freezing air and rain to swoosh around her in a strong swirl. She stiffened and worked to keep Flame going at his quick speed.

Please let no more cars come by, she prayed silently. *Let me get home.*

Up ahead, she saw an enclosed buggy going her same direction. It wasn't going at much speed, and she knew she couldn't pass it. Not in these conditions. Not in any conditions, really. It was too dangerous to leave their grooves on the side of the road to enter the regular lanes. Cars could come upon a buggy in an instant.

A sudden image of Eli's and Mark's accident filled her mind, and she squeezed her eyes shut.

Their district had already paid too high a price time and time again for sharing the road with motorized cars. She wasn't about to add to that toll today.

She pulled up on the reins, slowing Flame to his regular trotting speed, so they could follow the buggy safely, but he strained at his harness. Flame was a good horse, a steady and dependable animal, but that day he didn't seem any too pleased to slow his pace. He was just as anxious as she was to be home.

"Flame!" she hollered. "Let's calm down, boy. You're fine. I'm right here. You're fine."

She was afraid the wind had snatched her voice and the animal couldn't hear her, but he stopped yanking his head to the left and bore straight ahead. She was nearly on top of the back wheels of the buggy in front of her. She pulled up harder on the reins.

Did the person ahead even know she was behind them? The wind was howling so loudly by then, that she was sure the noise from Flame's hooves was lost in the melee. She just needed to bide her time. The sleet was caking on her lashes, and she blinked continually. She wished she'd put on her outer bonnet. It had enough of an overhang above her forehead to catch some of the icy rain, but as it was, she'd only worn her *kapp*, which was useless to keep anything from her face.

Her ears were freezing cold; indeed, they felt brittle. She wanted to readjust her scarf, but she was afraid to let go of the reins with even one hand. She was holding fast, keeping Flame under control. The buggy ahead of her surged forward, and she gasped with relief. If it would keep up that quicker pace, she could be home within fifteen minutes of so.

The sky darkened even further, and ice fell from the sky. The buggy forged a path ahead of her that seemed to help with her traction, and suddenly she was grateful it was there. She could think of nothing now but driving Flame—getting them both home safely. She clenched her teeth, and her breath came in shallow bursts of white air, puffing out before her.

"Come on, Flame," she whispered. "Keep on. Keep on. You're doing fine."

She had no sense of passing time. Her fingers were cramped now as they clung to the reins. She didn't feel the cold anymore. She was numb. When her drive appeared on the right, she nearly burst into tears. She drove Flame straight to the barn. She slid down from the cart and almost lost her footing on the iced gravel. With nearly-frozen fingers, she unhitched the horse and pulled him into the barn. She rubbed him down with a thick white towel and put him into his stall. She poured feed into his bucket and made sure he had water.

Before leaving him, Mary flung her arms around his neck. "Thank you, Flame. Thank you, boy. You got us home safe and sound."

For once, the goats didn't jump and fumble all over her. They were huddled together in the back corner of the barn, sensing the storm. Mary glanced at their cow, lazily chewing her cud and looking at her with sleepy eyes.

Mary ducked out of the barn and secured the door. She picked her way carefully back to the house, feeling the freezing rain seeping through the neck of her cape and dress. By the time she stomped her way over the porch and nearly fell inside the house, she was shivering violently.

The house was still and nearly dark. Why hadn't Mark lit the lantern? It was right there on the coffee table in front of him.

She shed her cape and her scarf. "Mark?"

No answer.

"Mark? Where are you?"

And then she heard it. A rustling sound. A moan.

"Mark!" she cried, really alarmed now. She darted into the front room and nearly tripped on him where he lay sprawled across the floor. She dropped to the floor beside him.

"Mark! What happened! Are you hurt?"

"I-I'm all right," he said, but his pinched tone belied his words.

She patted her hands over his chest and his arms, checking for injuries. "Did you fall?" She immediately realized the stupidity of her question. "Can you get up?"

She fumbled her way to the coffee table and lit the lantern. She held it high, looking at her husband. He wouldn't meet her eyes.

"I'm a darned fool," he muttered.

"What do you mean? How did you fall?"

He wouldn't answer her. His features were drawn, and she could see he was in pain. She went to him again and set the lantern on the floor.

"I'll help you up."

"I don't need your help."

The coldness in his tone slapped her, and she immediately jerked back. She had been on her haunches, and now she scrambled to stand up.

"B-but Mark…" She looked down at him, but he wouldn't meet her eyes. She hesitated, not sure what to do. She could hardly leave her husband collapsed on the floor—whether he wanted her help or not. And why didn't he want her help? And what had he meant about being a fool?

She waited. It was so still, she imagined she heard the ticking of the second hand on the clock in the kitchen as it jolted its way around the circle.

"Mark?"

He struggled until he was sitting. His breathing was labored, and his hand had gone to the cast on his leg, cradling it. He winced and shifted the cast a bit to the right. He glanced around as if looking for something to hoist himself up with. Mary let out a small cry and bent toward him again.

"I'm helping you," she insisted, her tone firm.

"I can do it." He gritted the words out.

"Well, maybe you can!" she cried, exasperated. "Maybe you can do everything in the world by yourself. Maybe you're one of those *Englisch* superhero cartoon people. I don't care! I'm helping you, and that's final."

She put her hands beneath his arms and pulled on him, but she had completely overestimated her ability and completely underestimated his weight. Mark hardly budged. She yanked on him again, bracing her feet into the floor and heaving with all her might. His weight was like a dead heifer. She let go of him and clenched her teeth.

His eyes were on her, unwavering, giving her a creepy feeling.

"Mark," she nearly shouted at him now. "You have to help me."

"I don't need your help," he repeated.

"Well, you obviously do," she snapped. "Now, I'm going to try it again, and if you can raise yourself even a little, I think we can do it."

She grabbed hold of him again, and he groaned. She drew back her hands. "Oh, I'm sorry! I forgot about your rib. Did I make it worse?" Remorse flooded her. In her stubbornness, she'd completely forgotten his cracked rib.

He shook his head. "*Nee*. You didn't make it worse."

She sank down on the floor beside him. "What is it?"

"I fell. I'm fine."

"You're not fine."

"I am."

His voice bit into her, and she flinched. The room was quiet again, and she didn't speak. Her mind whirled, trying to figure out what was going on with her husband. She'd thought they had made good progress. In fact, she'd been sure of it. So, what was this? What had gone on in his mind to make him so cold and bitter toward her now?

Chapter Thirty-Nine

Mary steadied herself. She was going to fix this if it was the last thing she ever did. She gazed at Mark. She studied his pained expression and the way his eyebrows drew down over his eyes. She looked at his strong shoulders and the way his muscles flexed as he held onto his leg. His sandy blond hair fell softly over his forehead. She wanted to touch him. Caress him. Snuggle into him.

She gave a start, realizing that he was watching her study him. She swallowed.

"I love you," she eked out, clearing her throat, trying to sound stronger, surer.

She felt the tightening in her chest, felt the deep ache swelling inside. Wouldn't he respond? Wouldn't he at least say something?

"Mark?"

He winced. "I heard you," he whispered. His forehead crumpled into a mass of wrinkles, as if he were trying to figure something out.

She held her breath.

"I…" he started. "I was worried about you. The storm…"

Mary blanched. She'd completely forgotten about the storm. She didn't hear the wind howling anymore, but she knew that snow and ice were often silent.

"You didn't come home as fast as I thought you would…"

"I was stuck behind a really slow buggy. And it was getting slippery, Mark. I couldn't go faster." Why did she feel like she had to defend herself? She didn't like it, and she didn't think she should have to defend herself. Without thinking, she backed away.

He must have noticed for his expression grew more strained.

He went on. "I fell when I was rushing to the front window to check for you."

She sucked in her breath. "I'm sorry," she whispered.

"The thing is, I wasn't just worried about the storm." He paused and seemed to be debating whether to tell her more. She waited.

"I thought maybe you… I thought that maybe…"

When he didn't finish, she leaned forward. "You thought that maybe I what?"

"I thought that maybe you and Isaac—"

She reared back, not believing her ears. "Me and *Isaac?* What do you mean?" Her sharp voice sliced through the air.

He sighed and his mouth formed a grim line.

"Are you serious?" she pushed out the words. "Me and Isaac?" Anger surged through her. "There *is* no me and Isaac!"

She was furious, and she knew she had to leave. She had to get out of the room before he said anything more to her. She couldn't bear it. She couldn't bear to hear her name linked with Isaac's again. And especially not by her husband.

She jumped to her feet. "I'll be in the kitchen," she said through gritted teeth. "Your supper will be ready soon."

She fled from the room and dashed into the kitchen, collapsing against the counter. She stood there, breathing hard, listening to her heart pound in her ears. How could he? How could he keep bringing up her former beau? What else could she possibly do?

She closed her eyes and willed her breathing to slow.

He'd thought she'd gone to see Isaac? To do what? Rush off into the storm together? How could he possibly think such a thing? Was he daft? And hadn't he already told Isaac to leave Hollybrook?

She heard heavy thumping, and she tensed. He'd gotten up. How? And now, he was coming. She turned toward the sink and stared into it. She couldn't see him right now. She was too angry.

"Mary?" he said from the doorway.

She bit her lower lip.

"I'm sorry."

Was he? Was he sorry? All Mary knew was that she was tired, sick-to-death tired of both of them being sorry. She was sick-to-death tired of tiptoeing around the house. She was sick-to-death tired of wanting to make sure everything was perfect for Mark so that he would forgive her. And not just for the Isaac mess. For their dead baby...their beautiful lost child.

She was empty. Completely empty. She didn't know if there was anything left to give.

She heard him move across the floor till he was standing behind her. She could feel his breath on her neck. A sudden chill made her shiver, and then his hands were on the backs of her arms.

"Mary." He turned her to him. She could see he was standing through his agonizing pain. His face was white, and his pupils were huge. "Please, come," he urged her.

He thumped his way to the dining table and sank onto one of the side benches. He leaned his crutches on the table and lay his hand on the spot beside him. "Please."

She swallowed against the tight lump in her throat. She stared at his hand, stared at the breadth of it, the callouses on his knuckles, the strength of his fingers. The hand that worked the land, cared for the animals... The hand that used to touch her with love. The hand that used to caress her face with tenderness.

She raised her eyes to his. His look of desperation rocked through her stomach, and she flinched. Could it be true? Could he really be sorry? She forced her feet to move. She forced herself to cross the linoleum floor of the kitchen and move into the dining area. She forced herself to lower onto the bench where his hand had been. But she could not, *would* not, force herself to look into his eyes.

"Please understand..." he started, and her insides began to scream. She didn't want to understand any-thing anymore. She didn't want to hear excuses, rea-sons, nothing.

He hesitated as if aware of the raging war inside her. "Let me start over," he said quietly. He touched her leg, and she flinched. He sighed heavily. "I've hurt you. I can see that."

She held her breath.

"I haven't trusted you." And there it was. *Finally.* Out in the open.

She looked at him.

"I haven't trusted you because I was jealous. Because I didn't believe that you loved me." He visibly swallowed. "I reckoned you were angry that I told Isaac to leave because you wouldn't want him to leave. You would want him to stay."

Tears burned her eyes, and she pressed her lips together, listening to his every word.

"I always knew he was a threat. I talked you into marrying me, and I felt guilty about that when he returned. I know he wants you back. I'm not a complete fool. And I know you would have gone back to him if not for me."

Mary's breath turned ragged. His words stabbed through her, and she worked to remain still.

"And then, when we lost the *boppli*… There was no reason for you to stay. I knew Isaac was trying to see you all the time. Stopping you on the road. On the *road*, Mary!"

She stared at his angry face and felt her heart go cold. But then, something happened and his face crumpled for a split second. She saw the agony in his eyes, but just as quickly, he regained his composure and continued.

"Losing our *boppli* about killed me. And somehow, we couldn't reach each other. I didn't blame you, Mary. Maybe, at first I did. Some. But not really. Not after I thought about it. I was hurting, and I blame myself for not making that clear to you. There was no blame. But I know you thought I blamed you for it." He sighed heavily. "I'm sorry. You were hurting, too, and I failed you in that."

She squeezed her hands together on her lap. He was right. He had failed her in that. She blinked hard and kept listening.

Chapter Forty

One of his crutches slipped from the table and clattered to the floor. Mark winced when he bent to pick it up. He laid it on the end of the bench and turned to her once again.

"When I learned about Isaac visiting you *again*, it about killed me. I was angry when I confronted him. Angrier than I've ever been in my life." He lowered his eyes. "I'm ashamed. Not for asking him to leave, but for my rage."

Mary tried to swallow, but her throat was too tight.

"I'm sorry that you're married to me, Mary. I would set you free, but that isn't our way. Divorce. It's not our way."

Divorce?

Had she heard him right? She blinked stupidly at him, trying to make sense of his words. Divorce? He was considering divorce? Didn't he love her?

Suddenly, as if the sky had opened, things became clear to her. The truth jerked through her mind and heart, and she scrambled up from the bench, facing him. It wasn't that he didn't love her. He believed she didn't love him. How had things gotten so bad, so twisted, so distorted?

"Mary?" he choked out, tears filling his eyes.

"You honestly think *I don't love you*?" she cried. "You honestly think I wanted to find Isaac today and *run off with him*?"

His eyes on her didn't waver. He squared his shoulders. "*Jah*. That's what I thought."

She shook her head, staring at him. *"We are both insane."*

His forehead creased, and she knew he was waiting for her to explain. She took a huge breath and wondered how much she should tell him. Should she be completely and totally honest? Wasn't that dangerous? Weren't some things best kept secret?

But as she looked into his eyes, as she saw his pain and confusion and vulnerability, as she thought back over the last three months, she realized that maybe, just maybe, the time had come. Look where they were. Look where her efforts to make things right had gotten them. What could be worse than this? What could be worse than pussy-footing around each other, trying to read each other's minds? Trying to put a nice sheen on a rotten crumbling floor?

She made herself take two slow breaths before she sat beside him again.

"All right," she whispered. "I'll tell you everything."

Dread crept over his face but he didn't flinch, nor did he draw away from her. Instead, he took both of her hands in his.

She began talking. "When Isaac came back, I was confused. And when he told me he wanted me again, it eased something in me. Something that had been broken inside me for years. He had hurt me so badly when he left. I never understood how he could have stopped loving me so easily. I yearned for him. I waited for him. And when he didn't return, I couldn't understand. I couldn't reconcile it with what we'd had together."

"I know that Mary—"

"*Jah.* I know you knew. So, when he came back, *finally*, and wanted me, well, in a way, I was at peace at last. There wasn't something wrong with me that had made him reject me for all those years. He still loved me—"

"He *left you*, Mary," Mark interrupted her, his voice tight. "He deserted—"

She pulled one of her hands away from his and held it up. "*I know that.* Don't you think I know that? But still, seeing him again, hearing him tell me that he wanted me back, did something to me. Inside."

Mark's face turned hard, and she knew she had to hurry.

"It was almost as if he healed me by coming back. He healed a hole in my heart." She shook her head. "Like I said, it confused me. And I will tell you the truth, Mark. I'm telling you everything now. You can turn me away if you want, but I'm telling you everything."

She wanted to plead with him to hear her, really *hear* her, but she was done with pleading. She was going to lay it all out and let whatever happened, happen.

"At first, I wanted him back. I wanted us to go back to the way we were before he left. I realized I still loved him…"

Mark sucked in his breath, but she didn't stop.

"…but then, I realized it was different. My love for him. I loved him for what he'd been to me in the past.

Not for what he was to me now. He wanted me back, but I didn't want him. Not like that anymore. At first, though, I thought I did. And when I lost our *boppli*…"

She paused, fighting for composure.

"When I lost our *boppli*, you weren't there for me. Oh, I know you tried to be, but you weren't. We failed each other during that time. I probably should have stayed home with you, but I couldn't. At the time, I just couldn't. I was dying inside, just like our babe had died. And I didn't know how to get over it. So, I fled."

Mark's eyes didn't leave hers, but she saw his grief as surely as he was seeing hers.

"When I returned, all I wanted was for us to be in love again. To be a couple. For you to be happy with me. I tried so hard. And I thought we were making progress."

He made a slight movement with his head, and she knew he was agreeing with her.

"But then, with your accident, I don't know what happened. You started pushing me away…"

"I wasn't pushing you away," he cried.

She touched his arm. "*Jah*, you were. You didn't want my help. You wouldn't let me in."

"I-I…"

"You wouldn't let me in, Mark. And there's something else…" She paused and licked her lips. "When you admitted that you'd told Isaac to leave…?" She shook her head. "When you told me that, I was relieved. *Relieved.* Do you hear me, Mark?"

His lips parted, and he stared at her.

"You have been so busy assuming you know everything about me that you haven't heard me. You haven't really *seen* me for weeks."

His eyes widened, and she shook her head again. "I'm

tired, Mark. I'm tired of fighting you and my past and my grief. I give up. I've told you everything, and I'm not sure you'll ever believe me. But the truth is, I do love you. I want our marriage to be strong and to last forever. I want to try again to have a child." She looked around the room. "I want to fill this house with children. *Our* children."

She stood and threw her arms out. "So. There it is. The truth. All of it. And now, I'm finished. I'm so, so, *so* finished. I'm tired."

She left him there and walked up the stairs to their room. She pulled the top quilt back from their bed and laid down. She pulled her knees to her chest and flung the quilt back over herself and closed her eyes.

She'd done it now. Told him everything. She felt drained but at peace.

Now, it was up to him.

When Mary awoke, the room was completely dark. She blinked, wondering what time it was. It took her a moment to remember why she was lying in bed in her dress. When it all came tumbling back into her consciousness, she gasped. Where was Mark? She'd left him downstairs. But he hadn't called after her from the stairwell. He'd let her go. She clasped her chest. He had let her go.

"Mary?"

She jumped at the sound of his voice. Was he there? In the room? And why hadn't she heard him come in?

And then she saw his silhouette. He was sitting on the small bench to the right of the door. She sat still, staring at him.

"Come here," he whispered.

Slowly, she got up and moved across the room. He took her hand and pulled her down onto his lap.

"Your leg!" she cried. "I'll hurt you."

But he wouldn't let her up. He put his arms around her and drew her down to his chest. She heard the rapid thumping of his heart.

"I told you that I wasn't a complete fool," he murmured in her ear. "But I was. A complete fool."

He nuzzled her neck, and she held her breath, waiting for him to continue.

"I want you to know something." He drew away, and in the black of the room, she knew he was looking into her eyes. "I heard you today. And I see you now." He gave a low chuckle. "Even in the dark."

She smiled then, hearing something new in his voice. Something light and free and beautiful.

"I want to promise you something," he said. "*Nee*. I want to promise you two things." He took a deep breath. "I promise that I will never bring up Isaac's name again. I know it's over. It's been over, and I was a fool."

She gasped and felt something inside her shift ever so slightly.

He kissed her neck and drew back to continue. "And the second thing? I promise to always see you, Mary. To always hear you. Like I did today."

Mary burst into tears and threw her arms around him. The shadows covering her heart broke apart and joy bubbled up through her. Her crying turned to laughter, and she buried herself into his chest.

"Mary," he whispered. "Mary. Mary. Mary."

She clung to him as if she'd never let go. And then he was kissing her. Kissing her with such abandon and such passion that she opened her lips to him, raising herself to meet him kiss for kiss. He groaned and clutched her to him. She pressed her lips to his and felt a deep rumble in her stomach.

"Mark," she muttered thickly.

He pulled away. "What?"

"I love you."

He moaned and kissed her again, claiming her until she held no doubt that he loved her, too. Later, she wouldn't be able to figure out how he had done it. How he had moved across the room with her. But suddenly, they were lying together on the bed, holding each other, feeling the sweet promise of a future together.

A stronger future. A brighter future. A future filled with understanding and hope.

And a future that would no doubt include a passel of children—hopefully, many strong sons who would look exactly like their father.

And, of course, a daughter or two, who would look exactly like her.

* * * * *

About the Author

Brenda Maxfield's passion is writing. Nothing is more delicious than inventing new characters and experiencing the world through their eyes. She is blessed to live part-time in Indiana, a state she shares with many Amish communities. She finds the best spices, hot cereal, and cooking advice at an Amish store not too far away.

Brenda has lived in Honduras, Grand Cayman, and Costa Rica. With her husband Paul, she has two grown children and five precious grandchildren. She loves to hole up in her lake cabin and write—often with a batch of popcorn nearby. (And some dark chocolate on the side...) One of her favorite activities is exploring other cultures, and she can often be found walking the beaches of Costa Rica.

She loves getting to know her readers, so feel free to write her at: contact@brendamaxfield.com.

To find all her Amish Romances, visit: http://www.brendamaxfield.com.

Happy Reading!

Other Amish Romances by Brenda Maxfield

LOVE INSPIRED

INSPIRATIONAL ROMANCE

UPLIFTING STORIES OF FAITH, FORGIVENESS AND HOPE.

Join our social communities to connect with other readers who share your love!

Sign up for the Love Inspired newsletter at **LoveInspired.com** to be the first to find out about upcoming titles, special promotions and exclusive content.

CONNECT WITH US AT:

Facebook.com/LoveInspiredBooks

Twitter.com/LoveInspiredBks

Facebook.com/groups/HarlequinConnection